ERLE STANLEY GARDNER

- Cited by the *Guinness Book of World Records* as the #1 bestselling writer of all time!

- Author of more than 150 clever, authentic, and sophisticated mystery novels!

- Creator of the amazing Perry Mason, the savvy Della Street, and dynamite detective Paul Drake!

- **THE ONLY AUTHOR WHO OUTSELLS AGATHA CHRISTIE, HAROLD ROBBINS, BARBARA CARTLAND, AND LOUIS L'AMOUR *COMBINED*!**

Why?
Because he writes the best, most fascinating whodunits of all!

You'll want to read every one of them,
from
BALLANTINE BOOKS

Also by Erle Stanley Gardner
Published by Ballantine Books:

THE CASE OF THE BORROWED BRUNETTE
THE CASE OF THE BURIED CLOCK
THE CASE OF THE FOOTLOOSE DOLL
THE CASE OF THE SHOPLIFTER'S SHOE
THE CASE OF THE FABULOUS FAKE
THE CASE OF THE CROOKED CANDLE
THE CASE OF THE HOWLING DOG
THE CASE OF THE MYTHICAL MONKEYS
THE CASE OF THE DEADLY TOY
THE CASE OF THE DUBIOUS BRIDEGROOM
THE CASE OF THE LONELY HEIRESS
THE CASE OF THE EMPTY TIN
THE CASE OF THE GLAMOROUS GHOST
THE CASE OF THE LAME CANARY
THE CASE OF THE CARETAKER'S CAT
THE CASE OF THE GILDED LILY
THE CASE OF THE ROLLING BONES
THE CASE OF THE SILENT PARTNER
THE CASE OF THE VELVET CLAWS
THE CASE OF THE BAITED HOOK
THE CASE OF THE COUNTERFEIT EYE
THE CASE OF THE PHANTOM FORTUNE
THE CASE OF THE WORRIED WAITRESS
THE CASE OF THE CALENDAR GIRL
THE CASE OF THE TERRIFIED TYPIST
THE CASE OF THE CAUTIOUS COQUETTE
THE CASE OF THE SPURIOUS SPINSTER
THE CASE OF THE DUPLICATE DAUGHTER
THE CASE OF THE STUTTERING BISHOP
THE CASE OF THE ICE-COLD HANDS
THE CASE OF THE MISCHIEVOUS DOLL
THE CASE OF THE DARING DECOY
THE CASE OF THE STEPDAUGHTER'S SECRET
THE CASE OF THE CURIOUS BRIDE
THE CASE OF THE CARELESS KITTEN
THE CASE OF THE LUCKY LOSER
THE CASE OF THE RUNAWAY CORPSE
THE CASE OF THE RELUCTANT MODEL
THE CASE OF THE WAYLAID WOLF
THE CASE OF THE MOTH-EATEN MINK
THE CASE OF THE LUCKY LEGS
THE CASE OF THE HALF-WAKENED WIFE
THE CASE OF THE DEMURE DEFENDANT
THE CASE OF THE SLEEPWALKER'S NIECE
THE CASE OF THE SULKY GIRL
THE CASE OF THE SINGING SKIRT
THE CASE OF THE SUBSTITUTE FACE
THE CASE OF THE FAN-DANCER'S HORSE
THE CASE OF THE NERVOUS ACCOMPLICE
THE CASE OF THE FUGITIVE NURSE
THE CASE OF THE GREEN-EYED SISTER
THE CASE OF THE HESITANT HOSTESS
THE CASE OF THE ANGRY MOURNER
THE CASE OF THE DROWNING DUCK
THE CASE OF THE QUEENLY CONTESTANT
THE CASE OF THE AMOROUS AUNT
THE CASE OF THE BLONDE BONANZA
THE CASE OF THE LONG-LEGGED MODELS
THE CASE OF THE DROWSY MOSQUITO

The Case of the
Screaming Woman

Erle Stanley Gardner

BALLANTINE BOOKS • NEW YORK

Copyright © 1957 by Erle Stanley Gardner
Copyright renewed 1985 by Jean Bethell Gardner & Grace Nago

All rights reserved under International and Pan-American Copyright Conventions. Published in the United States of America by Ballantine Books, a division of Random House, Inc., New York, and distributed in Canada by Random House of Canada Limited, Toronto.

Library of Congress Catalog Card Number: 57-5145

ISBN 0-345-37875-X

This edition published by arrangement with William Morrow and Company, Inc.

Manufactured in the United States of America

First Ballantine Books Edition: December 1994

10 9 8 7 6 5 4 3 2 1

Foreword

The more I study murder cases in real life the more I am impressed with the work being done by the leaders in the field of legal medicine.

Take my friend Dr. A. W. Freireich, for instance. He is a warm, friendly man. We all know him affectionately as "Abe," but formally he is A. W. Freireich, M.D., a Diplomate of the American Board of Internal Medicine, a Fellow of the American College of Physicians, Director of the Division of Internal Medicine at Meadowbrook Hospital in Nassau County, New York, Assistant Professor of Clinical Medicine at the New York University Post-Graduate School, Past President of the American Academy of Forensic Sciences.

More specifically, if you take an overdose of barbiturates (sleeping pills), sink into a coma and are at the point of knocking on the pearly gates, you will be brought back to the grim realities of mundane life (if they get to you in time) because Dr. Freireich had the daring, the imagination and the background of knowledge to administer the first intravenous injection of benzedrine sulphate to a dying girl of nineteen. The treatment brought her back to consciousness and established a new technique for combatting barbiturate poisoning.

In murder cases, it was Dr. Freireich who analyzed the small bottle of whisky from which Judd Gray tried to drink when he was being brought back from Syracuse by the New York City Police. The fact that this whisky had been loaded with mercury went a long way toward implicating Ruth Snyder in that famous case.

Many times when ingenious defense counsel had thought up ideas intended to influence jurors into finding murderers completely blameless, the presence of Dr. Freireich on the witness stand or seated at the side of the prosecuting attorney effectively hampered the verbal embellishments so necessary in making such ideas seem plausible.

In one case, the theory of the defense was that the murderer had been suffering from lead poisoning. Since he had been drinking heavily the night before it was claimed this caused an acidosis which brought about the release of lead from its storage place in the bones, giving the defendant "acute mania." This was most plausibly presented to the jury. Dr. Freireich, however, was able to show that the defendant didn't have lead poisoning in the first place, thereby dealing the theory and the defendant's hopes of acquittal a body blow.

In another case the murderer had cut the throat of the five-year-old child of a neighbor and sought to escape punishment by claiming a condition of "hypoglycemia" but overlooked an essential fact of bodily chemistry which Dr. Freireich was able to point out to the prosecuting attorney. The result was to establish the fallacy of the defense reasoning to the satisfaction of the jury which promptly returned a verdict of first-degree murder.

However, the main thing about Abe Freireich which appeals to all who know him is the warm, human friendliness of the man. He is never upstage. He never surrenders to petty jealousies and one never hears any criticism coming from his lips. Despite his vast knowledge he tries to create the impression that he is after all a very ordinary individual. At such meetings as those of the American Academy of Forensic Sciences, he is known for his warm handclasp and friendly grin. And when a mystery writer needs some bit of medical knowledge which is hard to find in textbooks, Abe

Freireich will sit down and patiently explain the obscure bits of poison lore which have somehow eluded the "authorities on the subject."

So I dedicate this book to my friend:

A. W. FREIREICH, M.D., F.A.C.P.

Erle Stanley Gardner

Chapter 1

Della Street, Perry Mason's confidential secretary, entered Mason's private office, walked over to the lawyer's desk and said, "You always like something out of the ordinary, Chief. This time I have a lulu!"

"Unusual?" Mason asked, looking up from the papers on his desk.

"Unique," she said.

"Give," Mason told her.

"A Mrs. John Kirby telephoned," Della Street said, "and wanted to retain you to cross-examine her husband."

"A divorce case?" Mason asked.

"No, she and her husband are good friends."

"Yet she wants me to cross-examine him?"

"That's right."

"About what?"

"About where he was last night."

Mason frowned. "Della, I'm not a lie detector. I'm not a psychoanalyst. I don't handle cases involving domestic relations."

"That's what I told Mrs. Kirby," Della Street said. "She told me she only wanted her husband's interests protected. She said she wanted you to listen to his story, puncture his self-assurance, and rip him to pieces."

"To what purpose?"

"She didn't say. I told her to call back in five minutes, and—This is probably the call," Della Street said as the telephone on her secretarial desk rang noisily.

"I'll talk with her," Mason decided.

1

Della Street picked up the receiver, said, "Hello. Yes, Mrs. Kirby. . . . Yes, Mr. Mason will talk with you."

She nodded to Mason who picked up the phone on his desk, said, "Hello, this is Mr. Mason talking."

Mrs. Kirby's voice was well modulated, and entirely different from the strident, emotionally surcharged tones Mason had expected to hear.

"I'd like to have you cross-examine my husband," she said.

"About what?" Mason asked.

"About where he was last night."

"Why?"

"So he'll realize his story won't stand up."

"So you can reproach him, or get a divorce, or—?"

"Good heavens, Mr. Mason! Don't misunderstand me. I'm a very devoted wife. I love my husband. That's why I'm calling you. He told me a story. I don't want him to tell that story to anyone else."

"Why not?" Mason asked.

"He might get stuck with it."

"What's wrong with it?"

"You'll know when you hear it."

"And you want me to cross-examine him?"

"Yes."

"Why?"

"So he'll realize his story is absurd. I'm hoping he'll then tell you what actually did happen."

"And then?" Mason asked.

"Then," she said, "you can help him. He won't tell you the truth on the first visit, but after you point out the weak spots, he'll leave your office determined to plug up those weak spots. Then, between us I'm hoping we can straighten things out."

"Why?"

"So we can help him."

"Can't you tell him that you know he's lying and—?"

"No, no, Mr. Mason! Please! It has to be done my way. My husband's a sales expert. He can make people believe black is white, and he's not averse to trying if he gets in trouble.

"He's in trouble now, but he doesn't know it. In order to keep our marriage happy I have to be the devoted, credulous wife. Please, Mr. Mason!"

"But how are you going to get him to come in to see me?"

"Leave that to me."

"Very well," Mason said. "But understand one thing, Mrs. Kirby, I don't want you to interrupt, I don't want you to—"

"Oh, good heavens!" she interposed, "*I* won't be there."

"Very well," Mason said. "Send him in at two o'clock this afternoon."

"Thank you," she cooed. "Good-by, Mr. Mason."

Mason hung up the telephone and glanced at Della Street. "Well," he said, "there's a welcome interruption to an otherwise humdrum day. You certainly described that one, Della!"

She raised an inquiring eyebrow.

"Unique!" Mason told her.

Chapter 2

At one-fifty-five, Mason pushed aside the list of citations on which he had been working and said to Della Street, "That's enough of routine for one day, Della. Let's have a cigarette and see if John Kirby is on time."

Mason settled back in his swivel chair, lit a cigarette, laced his fingers behind his head and smoked for a moment in silence.

The telephone on Della Street's desk rang, and Della Street said, "Yes, Gertie, what is it?" listened for a moment, then said, "Just a moment and I'll see.

"Mr. John Northrup Kirby is here for a two o'clock appointment with Mr. Mason," she said.

Mason looked at his watch. "Two minutes early, Della. John Kirby may lie to his wife, but he keeps his appointments. Tell Gertie to get his address and phone number, then to send him in."

Della Street relayed the instructions to the receptionist, then rose and went to wait at the door of Mason's private office.

"Hello, Mr. Kirby," she said after a few moments, "I'm Della Street, Mr. Mason's confidential secretary. Step right this way, please."

She stood to one side, and a big, bluff man with a jovial grin came breezing into the office, said, "Well, well, well, how are you, Mr. Mason? I've heard so much about you and about your cases. It's a real pleasure!"

Mason extended his hand which was promptly gripped by strong, stubby fingers.

4

"Sit down, Mr. Kirby," Mason said.

Kirby was in his early forties, a thick-necked individual with heavily colored cheeks, thin dark hair, and the breezy positive manner of a man whose personality is never at rest for a moment but is always vigorously asserting itself.

"Well, Mr. Mason, I suppose you wonder why I'm here." Kirby let his expansive smile include Della Street.

"The truth of it is," Kirby went on, "I'm wondering myself what the devil I'm doing here. My wife told me I should see a lawyer. I finally agreed to run up and have a talk with you just to keep peace in the family. So she made this appointment for two o'clock. But when you come right down to it, Mr. Mason, there's just no reason on earth why I *should* see a lawyer."

"Except to keep peace in the family," Mason said.

"That, of course." Kirby grinned. "After a while that becomes mighty damned important. Well, Mr. Mason, I know you're busy. I know you're terribly busy. I'll begin right at the start. It was something that happened last night and I just can't understand why my wife should feel— However, there's no use going into that. I'll just begin at the beginning and tell you exactly what happened."

"Go ahead," Mason said. "Do that."

"Well, we had a sales meeting last night. I'm president of the Kirby Oilwell Supply Company, Mr. Mason, and we have these get-togethers every once in a while when we bring up the problems of sales resistance and things of that sort."

"And something happened at this sales meeting?" Mason asked. "Something that caused you to—?"

"No, no, no! Not at the meeting, Mr. Mason, it was after the meeting."

"I see. Go ahead."

"Well, we had this meeting out at a roadhouse. Yesterday was Monday and this place is usually closed Mondays, so there was no regular trade to bother with. We made ar-

5

rangements to have an exclusive on the place, charter the whole shebang just for our gang."

Mason nodded his understanding.

"I was driving home, Mr. Mason. The reason I mention this roadhouse is that it was quite a ways out and I was driving back home when I saw this girl on the road."

"Driving?" Mason asked.

"Walking, Mr. Mason, carrying a one-gallon, red gasoline can. Well, of course you know what that means, and I stopped instantly. Some poor girl who had run out of gas and had to walk to a service station and was coming back to her car."

Mason nodded.

"I'll admit that right after I came to a stop, Mr. Mason, I had a qualm, a little misgiving. I understand that holdup men sometimes use a girl for bait, but this girl was walking right along, not standing in one place. She seemed to be minding her own business, and she looked like a real little lady, a very nice refined young woman."

"How old?" Mason asked.

"Oh, twenty-two or so. Something like that. Young, good-looking, well dressed, the kind of a girl who would be driving a good car."

"Go on," Mason said. "You picked her up. What happened?"

"Well, I picked her up. She had this one-gallon can of gasoline. I asked her where she was going, and she said just about a quarter of a mile farther, that her car had run out of gas, and she'd had to walk back to the gas station."

"Go on," Mason said.

"Well, I just sort of crawled along looking for this car of hers, and we covered half a mile and there was no car. Then we covered a mile and there was no car. I asked her how come, and she said she couldn't understand it, and then we came to a gasoline station. Well, of course she knew that she'd left her car between where I picked her up

6

and *that* gasoline station, so we turned around and went back.

"I drove back to where I *thought* I'd picked her up. Then, so there'd be no chance of a mistake, I kept right on until I came to the service station where she'd bought the gas. Then I turned around, took the extreme right-hand side of the road and just barely crawled along. I kept my headlights on high so they showed every bit of the side of the road."

"No car?" Mason asked.

"No car."

"So then what did you do?" Mason asked.

"Then I questioned the girl. She told me she'd taken the keys out of the car and put them under the rubber floor mat. Then she'd walked back to this service station, told them her story, got a gallon can of gasoline, and had started back to the car. She said the tank was just absolutely bone dry, that the car wouldn't go another foot without gas.

"Well, of course, Mr. Mason, there was no question about it by that time. Someone had stolen the car—either someone who had siphoned off gas and put it in the tank and driven off, or someone who had simply put a tow chain on the car and gone off with it."

"You notified the police of course?" Mason asked.

Kirby shifted his position. "Now there's the reason that my wife thought I'd better talk to a lawyer. I didn't."

"Why not?"

"She didn't want me to."

"Why?"

"Now there's something she wouldn't tell me, Mr. Mason. But here was this young woman—one of the most pathetic situations I've ever encountered. She didn't have a dime to her name. She—"

"How about a purse?" Mason asked.

"She'd left the purse in the car. She said there wasn't a great deal of money in the purse. She'd taken out a dollar

7

bill, enough to pay for the gas and had put that in her stocking. She said she didn't want to carry the purse in one hand and the gasoline can in the other as she walked back—"

"She walked back, not ahead?"

"That's right, Mr. Mason. She said she remembered having passed a gasoline station not more than half or three-quarters of a mile back. It had been a Shell station and she was carrying a Standard Oil credit card. She liked to buy all of her gasoline on that credit card and, while she knew her tank was low, she thought she had enough for another eight or ten miles. She thought she could get into town easily, and she was looking for a Standard station. Then the motor started to cough and sputter, and the car ran completely out of gas. She used the last of her momentum to pull over to the side of the road."

"She got it completely off the highway?"

"Got it completely off the highway. There was a place where she could get clean over onto a turnout by the side of the road."

"And then what happened?"

"Then she walked on back to the service station."

"Didn't she catch a ride?"

"No, it was only half a mile or so, and she was a little frightened about riding with strangers."

"Yet she rode with you all right?"

"She explained that. She said that when she walked up to the gasoline station she was walking on the side of the road, out on the gravel, but after she got the can of gasoline—it was only a gallon can but it began to get heavy, so then she started walking on the pavement. She said that she was getting a little weary and—well, something about my appearance seemed to reassure her. She told me that I seemed like what she called a 'Good Joe'—a nice compliment from a young woman like that. Believe me, she had class stamped all over her."

8

"What eventually happened?" Mason asked.

"Well, I naturally didn't know what the devil to do. Here was this girl who had just had her car stolen, no purse, no driving license, credit card, social security number—"

"You got this girl's name?" Mason asked.

"Oh yes, we got quite friendly. Now don't misunderstand me, Mr. Mason, but I'm just trying to tell this thing the way it happened."

"What was her name?"

"Lois Wagner."

"She was a working girl? Married? Single? What?"

"Well, I gathered she'd been married and divorced. She was a little reticent about telling me her personal history, and under the circumstances I didn't feel like pressing an inquiry. You understand, Mr. Mason, it doesn't take very long to drive a couple of miles looking for a car, and . . . oh, I suppose she was in the car with me for perhaps ten or fifteen minutes in all. I told her that she certainly should notify the police and give a description of the car, and she said, no, she didn't want to do that. So then I asked her what she was going to do, and she said frankly she had no idea. I asked her if she had any friends in the city, and she said she didn't know a soul. So I said, 'Now, look here, young lady. I'm not going to have you wandering around at night.' She pointed out that she didn't have any money, and I told her nevertheless I wasn't going to turn her loose to wander along the road."

"I see," Mason said dryly.

"Of course, Mr. Mason, I detect a certain note of skepticism in your voice, and I admit I felt the same way. I just had the feeling along toward the last that it was some sort of a game where she was bait or a decoy and—Well, I'm in a business where I have to do a lot of entertaining here and there, and I never know when I'm going to be traveling around, so I always carry quite a large sum of money with me."

"What do you mean, a large sum of money?" Mason asked.

"Well, I keep a thousand dollar bill concealed in the back of my card case, and then I have a wallet that usually has around seven hundred and fifty to fifteen hundred dollars in it. I try to carry four or five hundred-dollar bills all the time."

"I see," Mason said. "And you had money with you last night?"

"Oh yes."

"About how much?"

"Oh, I'd say around two thousand dollars. Well, anyway, I took this girl to a motel and told the proprietor I wanted a room for her, and—well, damn it! He wouldn't let me have one."

"Why not?"

"Suspicious, I suppose. Of course the idea of a single girl coming in that way with an older man and—damn it! He had a sign out that said *'Vacancy'* just as plain as could be, yet he had the crust to tell me that he didn't have any vacancies, that everything he had, had been reserved in advance."

"So what did you do?"

"Well, I explained to Miss Wagner that—it was a rather embarrassing situation."

"Go on," Mason said.

"So she suggested that perhaps if I'd register as husband and wife then we could get a room all right and she could stay in the room and I could go on. She was a very, very good sport about it. Of course she felt all broken up over the theft of the car and the loss of her purse and her personal baggage and all that, but she seemed most considerate and understanding, and she was afraid she was delaying me, afraid that she was making a terrific nuisance out of herself."

"What time was this?" Mason asked.

"Along about midnight. The sales meeting broke up a little after eleven, and oh, I suppose it was right around midnight."

"All right," Mason said, "so she suggested that you register as husband and wife, and what did you do?"

"Well, I went on to the next motel we came to. That was the Beauty Rest Motel. I drove in and said I wanted accommodations, and the manager just gave us a quick look and said, 'Twenty dollars,' so I registered."

"How did you register?" Mason asked. "Under your own name?"

"No, sir, I didn't, Mr. Mason. You see her name was Wagner, so I registered as Mr. and Mrs. John Wagner, and well, I'd forgotten to find out what city she was from, so I put down the first thing that came in my mind—San Francisco, California—and gave the first address that popped into my head. And then the registration blank provided for the license number of the automobile and the make of the automobile. Well, of course, I put down the make and I put down the first three letters of my license number and the first digit. Then I got smart and put down two phony numbers for the last two.

"By that time I was doubting the wisdom of what I was doing."

"I can well understand that," Mason said.

"Well, it was all right, Mr. Mason. I didn't know for a minute, but I thought perhaps there was going to be a catch in it somewhere, but there wasn't. I put up the money for the cabin, the manager took us down and showed us the cabin, and I parked the car and told Miss Wagner good night. I told her I wished she'd let me call the police, about the car, but she said there were reasons that she couldn't explain, and she simply didn't want the police brought in on the case. So I gave her ten dollars, told her good night, and went on home."

"What time did you get home?"

"Sometime around one o'clock or so. I didn't look at my watch."

"And your wife?"

"My wife was in bed."

"She woke up when you came in?"

"Oh yes, she woke up and asked a few questions about the meeting."

"You told her about Miss Wagner?"

"Not last night, no. I didn't tell her that until this morning. My wife is a frightfully good sport, Mr. Mason. She's been around salesmen and sales meetings and all that, and she's broad-minded and tolerant and she was laughing a little about the way we call these meetings to discuss new numbers in the catalogue and always wind up with the same old strip tease. She asked me if the meeting wasn't a little later than usual. So then I told her about this girl and she became very sympathetic. She said I should have brought her to the house, and insisted that I go back to the Beauty Rest Motel and see if we couldn't do something for her."

"You went back?"

"Yes. My wife went with me. We drove right up to the unit that had been rented to us, Unit Number 5, and the key was in the door. I went inside. The bed had been slept in, but there wasn't any sign of the young woman."

"Then what?"

"That's all there is, Mr. Mason. That's the story. She simply got up early, left the key in the door, and took off.

"My wife is afraid I may have let myself in for something. Of course charging me twenty dollars for a motel room for two people shows the manager of the motel was suspicious when we registered. I couldn't help that. I wanted to get on home, so I paid the twenty bucks. I'd have paid twenty-five if he'd said twenty-five."

"And so?" Mason asked.

Kirby spread his hands apart in an eloquent gesture. "That's it, Mr. Mason. That's the whole story."

"Well, that's a very interesting story," Mason said. "It's rather an unusual adventure! By the way, does your wife believe the story?"

"Why, of course she does. Why shouldn't she?"

"You didn't notice any skepticism on her part?"

"Of course not. Why the devil should she be skeptical? What is there that doesn't sound right? It's the truth."

"She wanted you to see a lawyer?"

"Only so I could be protected in case there was any—well, in case it was sort of a frame-up. After all, this girl may show up later on and try to make trouble over that husband-and-wife registration.

"Not that she could really do anything. My wife has absolute confidence in me, Mr. Mason. She knows I'm telling the truth."

Mason glanced at Della Street. "When you first noticed this woman she was carrying a red gasoline can?"

"That's right."

"A one-gallon can?"

"Yes, sir."

"The kind that are issued by service stations to people who have run out of gas?"

"Yes, sir."

"How was she dressed?"

"Oh, I don't know, Mr. Mason. I don't think a man notices a woman's clothes very much. She had some kind of a gray outfit. I remember a gray skirt, and I think brown shoes and stockings."

"Flat-heeled shoes?"

"No, sir. Very nicely cut shoes."

"High-heeled?"

"Fairly high heels. Nice alligator shoes."

"Now when you got to the motel," Mason said, "you

13

quite naturally didn't leave the gallon can of gasoline with her?"

"No, sir, I didn't. I— That would have been rather absurd to have put a girl off at a motel without a purse, or a toothbrush, or anything, and left her a gallon can of gasoline."

Kirby laughed nervously.

"Then," Mason said, "the gallon can of gasoline must still be in your car?"

"Well, yes. Of course. I guess it is."

"Where is your car now?"

"Down in the parking lot."

Mason said, "I'll go down with you, and we'll take a look at that gasoline can. Perhaps that will tell us something."

"Well," Kirby said, running his hand over the thin hair which swept back from his forehead, "come to think of it, Mr. Mason, I don't remember seeing that gasoline can in the car this morning."

"You don't!"

"No."

"Do you keep your car in a garage at your house?"

"Yes, sir."

"A double garage?"

"A three-car garage."

"Do you have a chauffeur or anyone who works on the cars?"

"No, sir, not regularly."

"Then who could possibly have taken the can out of the car?"

"Mr. Mason, I don't know. I . . . to tell you the truth, I just don't know what did happen to that can of gasoline."

Mason said, "I'd better look up the automobile registration and find out about the car that's registered in the name of Lois Wagner. We'll check back and find out what dealer

14

sold her the car, and in that way we can get a description of the car and—"

"Now wait a minute, Mr. Mason," Kirby interrupted, "you're going pretty fast on this thing."

"You're consulting me as an attorney," Mason pointed out.

Kirby cleared his throat, ran a finger around the inside of his collar. "It looks to me as though you're trying to break down my story."

"Break it down," Mason exclaimed. "Why there's nothing wrong with the story, is there?"

"Certainly not!" Kirby said stiffly. "Only you're making it sound as though I was trying to . . . to make an alibi in a murder case, or something. Good heavens, is that clock right?"

"Yes."

"Then I'm way off! My watch must be running half an hour behind. I have another appointment, a *very* important appointment, and I'm late for it."

Mason said, "If you watch is off, Kirby, you must have come half an hour early for your appointment with me."

"Well . . . yes . . . I wanted to be sure to be here. Well, thanks a lot, Mr. Mason. I'll call you later on. I'm terribly sorry! I'll be seeing you."

He was out of his chair and through the door all in one motion.

Della Street looked at Perry Mason.

"Well?" the lawyer asked.

"He is now on his way to buy a one-gallon gasoline can," Della Street said. "And then he'll have to paint it red and batter it up a bit."

Mason grinned. "By this time he realizes his story won't stand up, Della."

Della Street frowned, said, "I've heard that name somewhere before. Something that keeps trying to register in my mind. I—Good heavens!"

Mason raised his eyebrows.

Della Street's eyes widened. "Chief!" she exclaimed. "It all fits in."

"All right," Mason said. " What is it, Della?"

Excitement made Della Street's words tread on each other's heels as she said, "Chief, driving in this morning I had the radio on in my car. I was listening to the news and the weather forecast and there was an item of local news about a Dr. P. Lockridge Babb, living out some place on Sunland Drive, who was assaulted last night, knocked unconscious and is lying in a critical condition at the hospital this morning.

"Neighbors heard a woman screaming, heard the sound of blows and saw a young woman running out of the house. As I remember it, the description was almost identical with this girl that Mr. Kirby picked up."

"That description doesn't mean much, Della," Mason said. "Neighbors could describe almost any young girl as having the same general appearance."

"I know, Chief. But now I know where I heard the name of Kirby. Police thought the assailant was someone who had made an appointment late at night with Dr. Babb. They felt the young woman was probably a narcotics user, and, after she had entered Dr. Babb's office, she slugged him with a heavy glass beaker, grabbed his supply of narcotics and ran out.

"So the police looked through Dr. Babb's appointment book acting on the theory that he wouldn't have let anyone in at that late at night unless there had been an appointment."

"How late?" Mason asked, his eyes hard with interest.

"Around eleven-thirty."

"All right. Go ahead," Mason said. "What about the appointment book?"

"There were two names on it. I've forgotten the other name, but I remember that one of them was Kirby. I wouldn't have remembered that if it hadn't been for hearing it this morning, and then again this afternoon. It's been ringing a bell with me all day—that there was something I should know about this client of ours."

Mason pursed his lips, drummed silently with the tips of his fingers on the surface of his desk. "Probably there's nothing to it, Della, but run down the hall to the Drake Detective Agency, and get Paul Drake to find out something about this Dr. Babb business. Look up the location. If the location is right, the time is right, the description is right and the name is right, it *may* be that we have a client who's in a serious predicament.

"Try and get John Kirby on the telephone. Ring his office and leave word that I want him to call just as soon as he comes in. Try and get Mrs. Kirby on the phone and tell her I want to get in touch with her husband. Let's check on this thing.

"Now be careful not to get Paul Drake all steamed up. Tell him it's just a routine matter we're checking, not a case in which we have a particular interest. Just ask him to get busy on the telephone, find out what the facts are, and then report to me. Get one or the other of the Kirbys on the phone just as soon as you've started Paul Drake working."

Della Street nodded and left the office.

Ten minutes later Mason was advised that John Kirby wasn't at his office, that the residence phone didn't answer and there was, therefore, no way of reaching Mrs. Kirby. Paul Drake had been contacted and would report as soon as he could get the facts.

Chapter 3

It was nearly four o'clock when Della Street relayed Paul Drake's report to Perry Mason.

"Dr. P. Lockridge Babb, also known as Dr. Phineas L. Babb, is sixty-two years old, a semiretired physician and surgeon, living at 19647 Sunland Drive.

"That location is within a few blocks of the Beauty Rest Motel where John Kirby took the young woman.

"About eleven-thirty last night, one of Dr. Babb's neighbors heard a woman screaming and the sound of blows. The sounds came from the doctor's house. Evidently there was quite a commotion. A general handy man and assistant who lives in back of the house over the garage was taking a shower at the time. The sound of the screams was loud enough for him to hear over the sound of the shower.

"He threw a towel around himself and ran down the stairs from his apartment to see what was wrong.

"The neighbors on the east, whose name is Dunkirk, heard the commotion and saw this girl run out of the house. They notified the police. Police got there almost within a matter of seconds. A radio car was in the neighborhood when the report was received.

"The officers found Dr. Babb lying unconscious on the floor. A heavy glass beaker had evidently been used as a weapon. It was lying broken into halves a short distance away.

"The Dunkirks saw this girl running out of the house. She's described as young, dark brown hair, dressed in just about the same way as the girl Kirby picked up. The inter-

18

esting thing is that Mrs. Dunkirk, who saw her, is certain that the girl was not carrying a purse. Her hands were empty as if she'd been in a struggle and had dashed out leaving her purse behind.

"I've been trying to get Mr. Kirby every few minutes. His office says he isn't in, and they don't know where he is. The number at the Kirby residence still doesn't answer. I've been calling there every ten or fifteen minutes.

"Police found the appointment book kept by Dr. Babb in his office. It shows that during the evening he had appointments with two persons: one by the name of Kirby, and one by the name of Logan. No initials are listed in the book.

"Dr. Babb is in a critical condition. He's still unconscious."

Mason asked, "Was there any sequence on these names, Della?"

"It's hard to tell," she said. "The appointment book is one that has a separate page for each day of the year. Then these pages are divided into hours and half-hours.

"If these times as shown on the printed page mean anything, then Logan's appointment was for eleven, Kirby's for eleven-thirty.

"Police are inclined to believe Dr. Babb paid no attention to the printed subdivisions showing time. There had been several appointments for the afternoon apparently simply grouped as a unit. Then there were these two appointments for the evening."

Mason digested that information, then sat for a moment in frowning concentration.

Abruptly he pushed back his chair and got to his feet.

"Grab some shorthand notebooks and plenty of pencils, Della. It may or may not be a wild goose chase, but if we're going to have Kirby for a client, we'll at least give him *some* protection."

Chapter 4

It was still some two hours before sunset when Perry Mason and Della Street drove past the address on Sunland Drive.

Dr. Babb's bungalow was set back from the street at the foot of a steep hill. Behind the bungalow was a two-car garage, with an apartment over the garage.

"The Dunkirks must live in that house up on the hill fronting on this other street. Can you see the name of that street, Della?"

"Rubart Terrace," Della Street said, peering at the road sign.

"All right," Mason said, "let's go talk with the Dunkirks. Then we'll have a chat with this handy man who evidently lives in that apartment over the garage."

Mason turned his car up the steep incline at Rubart Terrace, parked his car with some difficulty on account of the steep grade. He and Della Street climbed steps to the porch of the Dunkirk house.

A man answered Mason's ring.

"I'm Mr. Mason," the lawyer said with his most affable smile, "and this is Miss Street. Are you Mr. Dunkirk?"

"That's right," the man said without showing either hostility or cordiality, standing there in the door waiting for Mason to go on. He was a man in his early fifties, with sandy hair, bushy eyebrows, gray eyes, sloping shoulders and a stubby, sandy mustache.

"I believe it was your wife who telephoned the police?" Mason asked.

"That's right."

"Is she in?"

"Yes."

Mason gave the man his best smile. "We'd like to talk with her."

"What about?"

"About what she saw and heard."

"She's told the police."

"I understand," Mason said.

The man in the doorway let the conversation fall to a flat stop. The sound of a piano banging away at an old-time piece of jazz music came from the house.

Mason stood expectantly waiting.

From behind the man in the shadows of the hallway a woman's voice, sharp with excitement, said, "Is that Perry Mason, the lawyer?"

"How do you do," Mason called across the man's shoulders to the invisible woman in the shadows. "Yes, I'm Perry Mason."

"Well, for heaven's sakes!" the woman exclaimed. "The idea of you coming here! Why, I never expected to see *you* calling at *my* house. I saw you in court once. Motley, get away from that door. Come in, Mr. Mason. Come in."

Mrs. Dunkirk was heavier than her husband, probably a good ten years younger, a full-curved blonde who seemed to be gregariously inclined and who instantly took charge of the situation.

"You folks come right in. What did you say this young woman's name was?"

"Miss Street," Mason said, "my secretary."

"Oh yes, Miss Street, how are you? I'm certainly glad to meet you, and I guess you've already met my husband. He's a little resentful of all the interruptions we've had to put up with last night and today. Now come right in and sit down. I heard you say you wanted to talk about what happened last night."

"That's right," Mason said.

"'What's your interest in it, Mr. Mason?'"

Mason smiled and said, "A client of mine is somewhat concerned about Dr. Babb. You see he's a friend of the doctor's. They're trying to get things all lined up—"

"Oh, I see," she interrupted. "Well, after all, there isn't very much I can tell. Perhaps you folks would like to sit right down here by the window. That's where I was sitting last night when all this happened."

"You certainly have a nice view from this window," Mason said as she led the way to chairs.

"Yes, we just live around that window. Motley simply can't get away from it. He likes to sit and look out over the valley. He'll spend half the time here with his binoculars, watching birds and people and ... just browsing."

Dunkirk said, "You make me sound lazy. I worked hard, Mr. Mason, until I was able to retire a couple of years ago, and I don't aim to do any great amount of work any more. We've got enough to live on as long as we keep our expenses budgeted and don't spend our money traveling around."

His wife laughed nervously. "That's intended for me, Mr. Mason. I've been trying to get him to take a trip down through Mexico and then South America. He isn't much for traveling."

"When you're traveling, you're spending money," Dunkirk said.

Mrs. Dunkirk, trying to keep what was evidently a sore point with her husband out of the conversation, said, "Well, you want to know what happened. We were sitting right here, my husband and I, and we'd been sitting in the dark talking for a while. Motley had some pictures he wanted to develop. He's fixed up a darkroom in the basement. He went down and started puttering around with his pictures. I sat here waiting for him to come back.

"When Motley is in the darkroom and comes up in between operations, he doesn't like to have his eyes dazzled with bright light and then go back to his photography. So we sit here with the lights out, and because the lights are out we have the drapes pulled back. It's beautiful up here at night, Mr. Mason. You see Rubart Terrace climbs up quite steeply, and we can look right out over the top of Dr. Babb's house and garage. We can see strings of lights from the valley, and watch the lights of cars on the boulevard. I suppose we'll get tired of it after a while, but right now I prefer it to television. It's a moving panorama."

"I take it you haven't been here very long?" Mason said.

"Not long enough to take the view for granted as yet. I hope we never do. I think it's the most beautiful place we've ever lived in, and very healthful, too. We're up here above the valley, and the smog—we haven't had any smog at all, well, that is, not to speak of."

Dunkirk said tonelessly, "We haven't been here long enough to tell."

"Motley's cautious." She smiled at Mason. "Well, I am willing to take Dr. Babb's word for it as far as I'm concerned. Dr. Babb says this location is relatively free of smog and he's been here for more than ten years."

"You've been visiting back and forth with Dr. Babb since you moved here?" Mason asked.

"Oh yes. You see Motley knew Dr. Babb before we moved in. It was because of Dr. Babb that we got this place. He told us it was for sale and he thought it was a good buy."

Motley Dunkirk said, "Dr. Babb treated me eight years ago and did a good job of it. He's a good doctor."

Mason picked up the pair of powerful binoculars which were lying on a coffee table and held them to his eyes. "These are remarkably fine binoculars," he exclaimed.

"Aren't they?" Motley said. 'I think I'm pretty much of an expert on binoculars, and this is the best glass *I've* ever seen. They have an exceptionally wide field and very sharp

23

definition. Look at that cat down there in Dr. Babb's yard, Mr. Mason. What's that he's playing with?"

Mason turned the glasses on the cat. "Dr. Babb's cat?" he asked.

"No, it belongs to the people next door, the ones who live on the west of Dr. Babb, Mr. and Mrs. Grover Olney. We don't know very much about them. They're not inclined to be neighborly. I guess they're all right, but they keep very much to themselves."

"The cat seems to have a goldfish," Mason said.

"Well now, what do you know?" Mrs. Dunkirk said. "That's the first time that cat has caught one of those goldfish, but heaven knows it's put in enough time sitting there by the pool."

"The cat spends some time there?"

"Yes. The cat's quite a hunter. It's fascinated by the goldfish. It sits there by the side of the sunken garden for hours. Notice the way Dr. Babb laid that out. I think it's very artistic."

"Dr. Babb didn't lay it out," Motley Dunkirk corrected. "It's that handy man of his, Donald."

"That's right, Don Derby," Mrs. Dunkirk said. "He's quite a worker. He's always puttering around with something, like when he took out the strip of lawn that was in there. It really was too small to be a lawn, so he made a beautiful sunken garden with a pool for the goldfish and a little artificial stream running between ornamental rock walls. Notice the various colored rocks there, Mr. Mason. They came from all over the country. Whenever Don can get away for a few days, he brings home a collection of rocks. He likes to go out in the desert and prospect."

"For minerals?" Mason asked.

"Not minerals. Just rocks. I don't think he'd know one mineral from another, but I'm satisfied some of those rocks really have value. Some of them are just as heavy as lead.

24

Particularly the batch he brought home from that last trip. When was that, Motley? About a month ago?"

"I believe so," her husband said.

"Well," Mrs. Dunkirk said, "I know that you want to know what happened, Mr. Mason, and good gracious, I know what a busy man you are! I read about your cases. They certainly seem to be spectacular."

Mason smiled courteously.

"He *makes* them spectacular," Dunkirk said.

"Mrs. Dunkirk said, "Now just don't interrupt me, Motley, and I'll go right ahead and tell them the story."

Della Street opened her notebook, held a pencil poised over the page.

"Police asked me particularly about fixing the time," Mrs. Dunkirk said. "It's pretty difficult to fix something like that right down to the minute. I have to sort of piece things together. The light over Dr. Babb's porch was on. I'd been sitting here for a while with Motley. He'd put through one batch of pictures and there was another batch he was very anxious to get developed. He went down to the darkroom. That must have been right around eleven-fifteen. I decided I'd make a cup of chocolate. I went to the kitchen and made the chocolate, and came back to sit by the window, sipping the chocolate and soaking up the view. That was eleven-thirty as nearly as I can make an estimate."

She ceased talking for a moment and the piano music changed from jazz to classical.

Mrs. Dunkirk said by way of explanation, "That's my niece Gertrude. She's going to be with us for a few weeks. Young people these days are quite a handful. She has to be doing something all the time.

"She's going to be terribly upset about that cat and the goldfish. She loves those fish—spends a good part of her time sitting over there by the goldfish pool, hand feeding the goldfish. In just a few days she's managed to tame them."

25

"How old is your niece?" Mason asked.

"Sixteen."

"Did she see anything last night?"

"Heavens, no! She was playing away on that piano."

"She plays very well, although there's a certain—well a mechanical rhythm to her playing."

Mrs. Dunkirk laughed. "Of course there is. It's a player piano. That's one of Motley's most treasured possessions, a genuine antique. It was one of the old kind that works with bellows and strips of perforated paper but Motley has fixed it up with an electric motor. He has a whole library of the old pieces. Land sakes! Sometimes I think Gertrude's going to wear that piano out. She was in there last night playing it until after midnight."

"Could we talk with her?" Mason asked.

There was a sudden embarrassed silence; then Motley Dunkirk said, "I don't think it would be advisable. She didn't see anything."

"She's very shy," Mrs. Dunkirk said.

"And easily upset, intensely nervous," Motley went on.

Again there was a brief silence.

Mrs. Dunkirk said, "Well, now, let's see. Where was I? I was telling you about this girl. Oh yes.

"I saw this young woman come walking up the street. You know, it was rather late for a young woman to be walking around unescorted, and—well, I noticed her. I wondered who she was. I didn't think she was anyone who lived here in the neighborhood. I didn't have anything else to do or anything to watch, so I picked up this pair of binoculars from the coffee table—we always keep them right there where they're handy—and looked at her.

"And then she turned in at Dr. Babb's house, and I could see her very plainly as she stood under the porch light. She had on a gray plaid jacket with a bluish-green ruffled blouse, and brown shoes. She was wearing a gray skirt. She had dark brown hair. I couldn't see the color of her eyes. She didn't wear a hat, and—"

"Just a minute," Mason asked. "Was she carrying a handbag or a purse or anything when she went in?"

"Now that's something I can't remember clearly, but I don't think she was carrying a thing. I won't say for certain but that's what I think. I do know she wasn't carrying a thing when she ran out."

"Go on," Mason said.

"Well, this young woman went in there, and it wasn't very long after that before I heard this terrific banging. At first I couldn't imagine where it was coming from. I called down to my husband to see if everything was all right, but he was shut in the darkroom and couldn't hear me. I hurried to the front door. Just then the woman started screaming. She screamed twice. I waited until the screaming had stopped for a few seconds; then I ran and telephoned for the police. By that time, of course, I knew the sounds were coming from Dr. Babb's house. I told the police I wanted to report that a woman was screaming and glass was smashing and I could hear blows."

"And then?" Mason asked.

"Then," she said, "I hung up the phone and went back to the front door."

"Not the window?" Mason asked.

"Heavens, no, Mr. Mason! I was standing there in the front door. I wanted to hear and see what was happening and to get away from the noise of that piano."

"Was the porch light on? Here, I mean."

"No, the porch light was out but the hall light was on. It was dark in the living room. There was just a small amount of light coming from the street light up there on Rubart Terrace. The porch light was still on over at Dr. Babb's house."

"All right, what happened?" Mason asked.

"I saw that young woman come running out of that front door just as fast as she could leg it."

"It was the same young woman?" Mason asked.

"Absolutely the same."

"And what happened?"

"She ran away down the street. I started down to Dr. Babb's house so I'd be there when the police arrived and that was when I saw Motley coming up the stairs."

Her husband said sharply, "I told you not to say anything about that, Elvira."

She said, smiling at Mason, "Motley just doesn't ever want to get tied up in anything as a witness."

"Coming up what stairs?" Mason asked.

"Up the cement stairs," she said. "You see, Mr. Mason, there's that flight of stairs from Dr. Babb's place up to Rubart Terrace, and then there are stairs from the lower part of our lot down to the street. Motley heard the scream and started down to see if he could be of any help, and then decided there wasn't anything he could do, so he turned around and came back."

"Donald had run down from his place over the garage," Motley said by way of explanation. "There was no need for me to go on the rest of the way down after he arrived. You see I had that batch of pictures right in the critical stage. I'd started to go down—oh, I don't know, I guess I was about a quarter way down the steps. That must have been while she was telephoning, and then I looked up and I saw Donald Derby, the handy man, down there, with a towel wrapped around him banging on the back door, so I turned around and hurried back up to get to my pictures."

Mrs. Dunkirk laughed. "Donald had been taking a shower. He heard the screams and didn't even wait to dress. That was just before the police showed up.

"There certainly was lots of excitement. I knew that since I'd been the one who telephoned I should be there to tell the officers about this girl, so they wouldn't lose any

28

time. So I ran down the cement walk to Rubart Terrace, ran down to Sunland Drive, and over to the house and I got there just a short time after the police arrived. I told them about the girl, and after a minute or so one of the officers started right out in the police car looking for her, leaving the other man in charge of the premises."

"And where was the handy man?" Mason asked.

"They sent him back up to his place to dress. You see, he lives over the garage there, and he certainly has a remarkably nice apartment. It's just as comfortable as can be."

"Has he been with Dr. Babb for some time?"

"He's been with Dr. Babb ever since I got acquainted with the doctor," Motley Dunkirk said.

"You didn't talk with the police?" Mason asked him.

Dunkirk shook his head. "I was back in my darkroom by the time the police arrived, and, as far as I'm concerned, I want to keep out of it. I was a witness once, and I was never so disgusted in my life. They had me come to court four times, and every time there'd be a continuance. Then, when I finally got on the witness stand and told what I knew, the lawyer on the other side browbeat me and shouted at me and shook his finger in my face and as good as called me a liar every time I opened my mouth. I got so mad I could hardly talk. I went home and was so sick I went to bed.

"And the judge sat up there on the bench and didn't do a thing about it. He didn't say a word to that lawyer. Everybody acted bored about the whole thing."

"What kind of a case was it?" Mason asked.

"Just a little, two-bit automobile accident case," Motley Dunkirk said. "I get mad every time I think about it."

Mrs. Dunkirk said, "Motley dashed back up the steps, and dove right into his darkroom. He kept at work on the pictures. I talked with the police, and because I talked with them, and because I'd been the one who had seen what had

29

happened, they didn't bother to come over here or ask if my husband had seen anything."

"Well," Motley said, "as far as I'm concerned, the woman who ran out of the *front* door didn't have a thing to do with it. It was the other woman who is responsible for whatever happened."

"*Another* woman?" Mason asked.

"That's right. The woman who ran out the back way."

"I never did see her," Mrs. Dunkirk explained to the lawyer. "She must have gone out when I was telephoning the police, or when I was getting the front door open. I didn't see her at all. Only Motley saw her."

Mason's voice showed sharp interest. "You saw another person?" he asked Motley Dunkirk.

"That's right," Motley told him. "This person was a woman and she came out the back door. And I have an idea she came out the back door about the time my wife was telephoning to the police."

Mason frowned. "This doesn't give us a very good basis for a time schedule," he said.

"We just can't figure it out," Motley said. "I've been trying to compare notes with Elvira and it's hard to get things straight. You see when I got part way down those steps I couldn't see the front of the house. My wife, up on the porch and at the window here, could see both the front and the back of the house, but she went to the telephone. Then right after that she ran down the street to get to the front of Dr. Babb's house, and after she did that she couldn't see the back of the house.

"I wear bifocal lenses and stairs bother me, so I had my head down watching those steps, but I'd stop and look up once in a while, and I certainly saw this woman."

"You mean the woman who left by the front door and—?"

"No, no," Motley said impatiently. "I mean the woman who left by the back door."

30

"Tell me about her," Mason said.

"Well, the way I figure it, this woman was the one who must have knocked Dr. Babb out. That's the *only* way I can figure it."

"Can you describe her?" Mason asked.

"Nope. She was a woman and that's all I can say. She was wearing a coat—it came about to her knees, I guess."

"A hat?"

"I couldn't see, or else I can't remember. I just had a glimpse of her, Mr. Mason. The back door swung open and this woman came out on the run."

"Where did she go?"

"She took off around the house, running the other way so the house was between us. I only saw her for a second."

Mason fought to keep his face expressionless. "Then the police don't know anything about this woman you saw running out of the house?"

"That's right, Mr. Mason, they don't. You see they never did come over here. Elvira went over to Dr. Babb's house to talk with them. At that time she knew nothing about this other woman. She didn't tell them about seeing me on the steps. She just said I'd been down in my darkroom. You see, the way our house is built on a side hill, our so-called basement is built into the bank at the back but is sort of a ground floor on the street side. That's the way they do with this type of hillside construction in this country."

Mrs. Dunkirk said to Mason, "I'm worried about Motley not saying anything about what he saw. Don't you think he should report what he saw to the police?"

Mason looked over to make certain that Della Street's busy pencil was recording his words. "I certainly *do* think that your husband should advise the police. I think it is his *duty* to do so."

Dunkirk's laugh was dry and mirthless. "Anytime the police want to know what I saw they can come and ask me, and I'll tell them. I'm not looking for any trouble. I'm cer-

31

tainly not going out of my way to get my name mixed up in anything. As far as I'm concerned, I think Elvira has done too much talking already.

"Now I'm going back downstairs. I got some pictures washing down there. Might surprise you, Mr. Mason, but I won a first prize in a contest given by one of the photographic magazines this month, and I've got one of my pictures hung in a camera exhibition in New York right now."

"Good for you!" Mason exclaimed.

Mrs. Dunkirk's smile was maternal. "He's just like a kid with a new toy," she said, "but I think it's good for a man to have a hobby after he retires."

"It certainly is," Mason agreed, glancing at his watch, "and now I've got to be on my way. This was a most interesting interview. Is the hired man over there now?"

"I believe he is. The police are letting him use the apartment over the garage, but they've sealed up Dr. Babb's house. No one can get in."

Mason frowned. "Do they expect Dr. Babb to die?"

"I don't know. They won't tell anybody a thing."

"Well, we'll talk with the handy man," Mason said.

Mason and Della Street shook hands with the Dunkirks and descended the steps to Mason's car. The lawyer carefully backed out onto Rubart Terrace and eased the car into Sunland Drive, then parked again almost in front of Dr. Babb's house.

"How about this other woman?" Della Street asked.

"No one knows about her except Mr. and Mrs. Dunkirk, you and me, Della. And I'm certain your notes disclose that I advised Mr. Dunkirk to communicate his information to the police."

"I have a verbatim transcript of the conversation."

Mason grinned.

"Are you going to tell your clients?"

"I'll have to think it over, Della. Let's go talk with the handy man."

The lawyer, accompanied by Della Street, walked up the cement driveway past Dr. Babb's house, around to the back, and climbed the steps to the apartment over the garage.

Mason pressed his finger against a bell button to the right of the door, and after a moment the door was opened by a wiry, lean-waisted individual apparently in the late fifties.

"Hello," he said, "how's Dr. Babb?"

"I don't know," Mason told him.

The man's face showed disappointment.

"You're asking about what happened last night, aren't you? I saw you folks go up to call on the Dunkirks."

"That's right," Mason explained. "But I haven't seen Dr. Babb and haven't heard anything new about his condition. He was still unconscious the last I heard."

"Well, come in if you want," the man said. "What do you want?"

"We only wanted to ask you a few questions."

"Well, come on in."

Mason and Della Street entered a small two-room apartment. The door automatically clicked shut as their host explained, "I'm sorry you have to come in through the kitchen. I told Doc he'd built the whole thing backwards, but that's the way Doc planned it and that's the way it is."

"My name's Mason," the lawyer said as the handy man led the way through the kitchen to the other room of the apartment, a combination sitting room and bedroom.

Apparently the name meant nothing to the handy man. "I'm glad to know you, Mr. Mason," he said. "Just call me Donald, or Don. Everybody does. Have a seat, Mrs. Mason."

Mason shook his head and smiled. "This is Miss Street, my secretary."

"Oh! I'm sorry! No hard feelings. Sit down both of you. I'll sit on the bed. You folks sit in the chairs there. Now what was it you wanted to know?"

33

"Just what happened?" Mason said.

Derby shook his head. "I've been through it so darn many times," he said wearily. "All right. Here's what happened. I was taking a shower in there, and I heard—"

"Had you been here all evening?" Mason asked.

"Me? No, I'd been over with Doc. Doc works pretty late hours."

"Do you have regular hours?"

"I work when Doc works. I come over here when he tells me to go over to my place. He's apt to open that back door and call to me any time. He just whoo-hoos and I go over."

"Dr. Babb had a couple of appointments for last evening?"

"That's what they tell me. I didn't know. The police got his appointment book. They say there are two names in it: Kirby and Logan. Neither one of them means anything to me, but that's neither here nor there—although I've heard that name Logan somewhere before, been trying to think of it all day but can't quite make it. Never did hear the name of Kirby.

"Anyway Doc had got everything out of the way that was bothering him last night, so he sent me over here. Told me he wouldn't be needing me any more."

"What time?" Mason asked.

"I suppose that was about eleven o'clock."

"And you undressed and took a shower?"

"Not right away. I puttered around for a while with a few little things and got sheets changed on my bed. I'd left in a hurry yesterday morning, and had left the bed just the way I climbed out of it."

"Why the hurry?" Mason asked.

"Doc had something he wanted. Forgotten now what it was. He stepped to the back door and let out a yell for me. That's the way he is; when he wants something he wants it. I was up all right, and had had my breakfast, but I hadn't

34

straightened up around here. It was the day I change the sheets on my bed. I like to keep things shipshape and tidy."

"All right," Mason said. "You got into the shower. What happened?"

"I heard something that was shrill and sharp, and then suddenly I realized it must be a woman screaming. I shut off the water and ran over to the window, soaking wet. I was just in time to see the back door swinging shut. Doc had opened that back door to call to me all right, but he'd either changed his mind or somebody had jerked him back—probably stuck a gun in his ribs. I was just in time to see the door as it swung shut.

"Well, I knew Doc wanted me and I reckoned he wanted me right away. I knew something was wrong down there, so I dashed over and grabbed the towel and wrapped it around my middle."

"You saw the door swinging shut?"

"That's right. There's an automatic closing dodad on it. It would have shut the minute Doc stepped back inside the house."

"Did you see anyone come out?"

"Nope. I don't think any person could have gone out. I think Doc pulled the door open to yell for me to come over and someone must have stuck a gun on him and jerked him back. Anyhow that's what I *think* happened."

"Could he have called for you and you not have heard it because of the water running in the shower?" Mason asked.

"Nope, I don't think so. When Doc hollers he lets out one hell of a bellow. I'd have heard him. I heard that woman scream even with the water running in the shower, and she was inside Doc's house."

"How do you know that?" Mason asked. "Couldn't it have been a woman standing at the open door and screaming? She could have gone back inside the house just as you reached the window."

The handy man thought that over. He rubbed his hand

35

along his jaw. "Gosh yes!" he said at length. "When you put it that way, I guess she could. I'd been wondering about that door. If Doc had got it open, he'd have bellowed, and I'd have heard him."

"What did you do?"

"I grabbed a towel, ran down the stairs and banged on the back door for Doc to let me in. There wasn't a sound from inside the house. Everything was just as quiet as could be. That scared me. I started around to the front of the house, and stopped just long enough to tap on the side window, and that's when this police officer who had moved around from the front of the house and saw me standing there wanted to know what the hell I was doing and who I was."

"And then?" Mason asked.

"The other officer had gone in through the front door. It was open."

"You mean unlocked?"

"No, I mean partially opened. Anyhow that's what the officer said."

"Does Dr. Babb keep narcotics over there?" Mason asked.

"I wouldn't know. I suppose he does. Come to think of it I guess he has to."

"Do you have keys to the house over there?" Mason asked.

"Not me. Doc says this is my house and that's his. When he wants me over there he calls me. If he doesn't call me I don't come. That suits me all right. He can mind his business, and I'll mind mine. I'm working for him, and I try to do as I'm told and keep my nose clean."

"All right," Mason told him, "now I suppose you've talked with Mr. and Mrs. Dunkirk?"

"I've talked with her. I haven't talked with him."

"You heard her description of the young woman who was seen running out of the house?"

36

"Uh-huh."

"I am wondering," Mason said, "if perhaps this same young woman hadn't called on the doctor on other occasions."

"Perhaps, I wouldn't know. He didn't have many patients. He's sort of retired. I try to keep out of the way when there's a patient over there, unless Doc wants something. I help out once in a while whenever he needs a helper.

"Doc's a close-mouthed cuss. That suits me all right. He's trying to retire, you know. Say, wait a minute! I've got an idea. There may not be anything to it, but there's just a chance. I think this woman's name *was* Logan. She sure had class. She was over—let me see—it'd be Friday, Friday morning."

"Go on," Mason said.

"Well, now look," Donald said. "I was working out there on the goldfish pool you can see right down there out of the window when this girl drove in, in this nice, shiny Ford and asked me if Dr. Babb was home.

"Well, Dr. Babb doesn't pay me to give out information, and I said she'd have to go to the front door and find out. But she just laughed and honked the horn a couple of times, and pretty soon the back door opened and Dr. Babb came out and was glad to see her, and she got out of the car and went in.

"Now this dame was real class. She had chestnut-colored hair, and she had lots of this and that and these and those. At first I didn't like her so much because of the high and mighty way she'd acted when she asked me if Dr. Babb was in, but she sure made a hit with me after she came out. She stood around and wanted to know all about the goldfish and really made sort of a play to butter me up. I couldn't figure what she had in mind, but it was nice.

"She'd been driving this new car of hers with one of the temporary pasteboard license numbers pasted on the inside

37

of the rear window. She told me she'd just got her regular license plates. She said she was going to put 'em on, and it seemed the most natural thing in the world for me to volunteer to do it for her.

"Shucks! It wasn't anything that took over a few minutes and I was glad to do it, but she sure made a production out of getting me lined up so I'd do the job.

"Now *her* name was Logan. I remember she told me her last name. I can't think of the first name to save my life, but I do remember the license number on the plates. It was AAL 279.

"Now maybe that'll help. I don't know."

Mason glanced at Della Street. "Did the police ask you anything about whether you knew anyone by the name of Logan?"

"Sure they did. But I didn't tell them this because I hadn't thought of it at the time. It's just this minute popped into my head, and I still don't know whether it means anything or not, but I'm sure now that her name was Logan."

"It could be the same girl," Mason said. "How did it happen she drove her car into the driveway and stopped out here in front of the garage?"

"Hanged if I know."

"Had she ever been here before?"

"Not that I know of, but she certainly seemed to know Doc all right. I'd been away for four days earlier in the week and she could have been around here during that time all right."

"There's a young woman across the street," Mason said, "a niece of the Dunkirks. Do you know her?"

"You mean Gertrude?"

"Yes. Do you know her?"

Donald laughed a short mirthless laugh. "Sure I know her. She's over here off and on watching the goldfish, playing with the cat. Poor kid, I guess she has nothing else to do.

"She's a funny kid. If I'd been Doc I'd have sent her

peddling papers, but he sure puts up with her, feels sorry for her. She's hanging around all the time, and she'll go through that back door. If somebody opens that back door she'll dart in before it closes and be inside the house before a man can wink his eye.

"She acts like she has a case on Doc—wants to be around him all the time. She told me that Doc's the only one who really understands her. She has spells of being moody, that girl. I saw her a while back when she didn't know I was watching her. She was sitting there by the goldfish pool crying, not hard crying, just sort of weeping.

"I guess Doc's putting up with her on account of the Dunkirks. They're old friends of his. *They* say the girl is sixteen. For my money she's about fifteen. She's big and well formed, but you can tell the way she acts she's just a big, overgrown kid."

"Well," Mason said, getting to his feet, "I just wanted to drop in and talk with you. You've told me what I wanted to know."

Donald touched the lawyer's sleeve. "You don't know anything about how Doc's getting along?"

"No. I suppose you could telephone the hospital and—"

"I can't telephone from here," Donald said. "The house over there was sealed up by the police. They've put special padlocks on the door. They told me I could keep on living up here, but I know Doc wouldn't want me to go away under the circumstances. He'd want me to keep an eye on the place."

"You don't have a telephone in this house?" Mason asked.

Donald shook his head.

"Well," Mason told him, shaking hands, "we may be seeing you again. I'll try to find out how Dr. Babb is coming along, in case we drop in again."

"Do that," Donald said, "and come in any time. A fellow gets sort of lonesome just sticking around here doing nothing except reading and listening to the radio. And thanks a lot for dropping in, folks."

He escorted them to the door, and insisted on shaking hands with both the lawyer and his secretary.

"And now?" Della Street asked, as they descended the stairs from the garage.

"Now," Mason said, "we'll telephone Paul Drake."

They found a phone booth at a service station six blocks down on the main highway.

Mason dialed Drake's number. "Paul," he said, "I want a name and address from an automobile license and I want it quick."

"What's the number?"

"AAL 279," Mason said.

"Okay," Drake said, "give me three or four seconds to relay the request to one of my operatives and he'll get busy. Hang on for a minute, Perry, I've got something to say to you."

Mason held on to the telephone for some ten seconds; then Drake was back.

"Okay, Perry, I've got that in the works. Call me again in ten minutes and I'll have the information."

"All right, Paul, what was it you said you wanted to tell me?"

"You sent Della down to pick up information about a narcotics robbery, chap by the name of Dr. Babb?"

"That's right," Mason said. "What do you have on it, Paul? Anything?"

"The guy died about thirty minutes ago. They said that he recovered consciousness enough to answer questions. There's a rumor he gave the police information but that's all I know. They're not releasing any further information."

Mason thought that over for a minute.

"Okay, Paul, thanks," he said. "I'll call you in ten minutes."

Mason sprinted for the car.

"What is it?" Della Street asked.

"It is now a case of murder," Mason said, "and we may be just *one* jump ahead of the police. Paul said to call him in ten minutes and he'll have the address of the license number AAL 279."

"Where are we going now?"

"Over toward Kirby's house. If the automobile license pays off, we'll be that much nearer the center of the city. If it doesn't we'll swing over to Kirby's and see what we can find out there."

Mason drove for ten minutes, then stopped the car in front of a phone booth. "Give Paul a ring, Della."

Della Street entered the booth, telephoned Paul Drake and came hurrying out. "The name is Norma Logan. The car is a very late model secondhand Ford, and the address is Mananas Apartments."

"Atta girl!" Mason said. "The Kirbys can wait, Della. Let's go!"

Chapter 5

The directory by the side of the door of the Mananas Apartments showed that Miss Norma Logan lived in apartment 280.

Mason and Della Street took an automatic elevator to the second floor, found the apartment and rang.

The door was opened by a strikingly beautiful young woman with blue eyes and chestnut hair. From the interior of the apartment came the faint aroma of cooking.

"Yes?" she asked, in a voice that was pleasing to the ears.

"I'm Perry Mason, an attorney," the lawyer said.

For a moment she glanced away from him, then looked back.

"Yes?" she said again.

"You're Norma Logan?"

"Yes."

"This is my secretary, Miss Street, Miss Logan."

Norma Logan acknowledged the introduction with an inclination of her head and the faintest of smiles.

"May we come in?" Mason asked.

"I'm sorry. I'm just cooking dinner, and then I have to dress. I have a date tonight."

"We want to talk with you," Mason said.

"I'm sorry."

"About Dr. Babb," Mason said.

Again the eyes flickered away from Mason's, only to return. "Dr. Babb?" she asked, and shook her head. "I'm afraid I don't know any Dr. Babb."

42

"You did," Mason told her.

Again she shook her head.

"And about John Kirby," Mason told her.

"Kirby?" She repeated the name as though trying to test the sound on her ears. "I'm sorry, Mr. Mason, are you quite certain you have the right Miss Logan?"

"You're Norma Logan?"

"Yes."

"Then I'm quite certain."

"Well *I'm* quite certain there's some mistake. I don't know any Dr. Babb and I don't know of any Kirby. Kirby? I've heard the name somewhere but I certainly can't place any Kirby at the moment."

"Do you have a Ford you recently purchased?"

"Yes, if that makes any difference. And now I'm very sorry, Mr. Mason, but I have no time to stand here and discuss these matters. There's been some mistake and since I'm in very much of a hurry, I'm going to have to ask you to excuse me."

She started to swing the door.

Mason pushed his weight against it. For a moment, she struggled to get the door closed. Then she jumped back. "All right," she said angrily, "do you want me to start screaming?"

Mason, followed by Della Street, walked through the door.

"Close it, Della," Mason said.

Della Street closed the door.

"This is an outrage," Norma Logan blazed. "I'm going to scream . . . or I'll call the manager. I'll call the police. You have no right to do this."

"I think you'd better call the police," Mason said. "I think they're the ones who are interested and since they're going to have to be called in sooner or later let's have them in now."

She looked at him, white-faced, indignant and apparently badly shaken.

"What in the world are you talking about?"

Mason said, "I hate to bring bad news, but Dr. Babb died about an hour ago."

"I don't care if a hundred Dr. Babbs died," she blazed at him. "I don't know any Dr. Babb. What are you talking about?"

"And Mr. Kirby can't be found," Mason said. "I think the police will probably be taking a great deal of interest in some of these developments."

"So what?"

"Aren't you sorry Dr. Babb died?" Mason asked.

"I would be if I—" Suddenly she collapsed in a chair and burst into tears.

Mason sat down on the davenport.

Della Street promptly seated herself at a small table, took out her shorthand notebook and pencil.

"Now suppose you tell me what happened," Mason said, "but before you do so let's have one thing understood. I can't act as your attorney, and anything you tell me won't be confidential and it won't be privileged. I am representing someone else."

She raised frightened, tear-filled eyes. "There's been some terrible mistake, Mr. Mason. I *do* know a John Kirby, but I *don't* know Dr. Babb."

"Where were you last night?" Mason asked.

"I was driving my new automobile out in the northwest part of town. I thought I had plenty of gasoline, but I didn't. I ran out of gas and had to walk back to the service station."

"Go on," Mason told her in an expressionless voice.

"I got a gallon can of gasoline and started walking toward my car. A man by the name of Kirby picked me up. I had never seen him before, and I don't ever expect to see him again. He drove me to where my car had been parked."

When we got there the car was gone. Someone had evidently siphoned gasoline into my car and driven it away.

"Mr. Kirby was a perfect gentleman. He took me to a motel, registered me, and then went home without ... well, you know, without any passes or any fresh talk. He was just a wonderful gentleman."

"How very fortunate!" Mason said dryly. "And then what happened?"

"Then early this morning ... I ... well, I was worried and frightened, and I couldn't sleep, so I got up about daylight and walked down to the highway. A milkman, making early morning deliveries, picked me up and carried me in to where I could get a taxicab. I came home, and about noon I received a call from a roadhouse—the Purple Swan. They said my car was parked in the driveway where it was an obstruction, and would I please do something about it. I made sure it was my car."

"How did they get your name?" Mason asked.

"From the registration certificate."

"So you went out there and retrieved the car?"

"Yes."

"What was the name of the motel where you stayed?"

"I can't remember."

"Do you remember its location?"

"Yes, I'd know it if I saw it again."

"Well," Mason said, "let's check back a little. You're absolutely certain you don't know any Dr. Babb?"

"I'm positive."

"You never did know of him?"

"I never heard of him in my life."

"How long have you had your license plates and registration certificate on your new Ford automobile?"

"Not very long. Just a few days."

"Who put the license plates on the car for you?"

"Does that make any difference?"

"It might."

"I had it done."

"Who did it?"

"A friend who happened to be handy with tools."

"A handy man?" Mason asked.

"I suppose so. Why? What difference does it make?"

"It makes a lot of difference," Mason said, "because he happened to remember the license number. You see it was last Friday, and you were out at Dr. Babb's place. You didn't stop in front of the house, but drove your car right up the driveway and around to the back of the house. You stopped in front of the goldfish pool. You may remember the handy man was there. You used a little flattery, turned on the personality and got him to put on the license plates for you."

Her wide, pathetic eyes showed that she knew she was trapped.

"Now then," Mason said, "Dr. Babb is dead. He has been murdered. You were seen running out of the house. You have a short time before the police get here. I don't know how long. It way be a matter of minutes, it may be a matter of days, but they'll find you. You don't have to tell me your story. If you want to, I'll be glad to listen, but I'm representing someone else."

"I know whom you're representing," she said. "You're representing John Kirby. He told me if anything happened and you *should* be able to find me that I was to back up his story about the gasoline and the stolen automobile."

"When did he tell you that?" Mason asked.

"About half an hour ago."

"He was here?"

"No. He called me on the phone."

Mason's eyes narrowed. He glanced over to where Della Street's busy pencil was flying over the page of the short-hand notebook.

"Better tell me the whole story," he said wearily.

She said, "I'm Ronnie's half-sister."

"Who's Ronnie?" Mason asked.

"Ronson Kirby."

"Go on," Mason told her.

"He's the cause of it all."

"Any relation to John Kirby?"

"Don't you know?" she said. "He's the son."

"Go on."

She said, "Dr. Babb was running just the opposite of an abortion mill. He was running a baby mill."

Mason waited for her to go on.

"I uncovered it because I was interested in Ronnie. Otherwise I would never have had the faintest inkling of what was going on. Dr. Babb was awfully clever. He had two little private hospitals. One of them was a hospital where rich society women went, ostensibly to be confined.

"The other hospital was where unfortunate women went to be delivered of children they didn't want.

"Instead of going through the red tape of adoption proceedings and conforming to all of the laws in regard to adoption, Dr. Babb would simply fill out a birth certificate and sign it as the attending physician. That made the baby the legitimate child of the foster parents as far as the records were concerned.

"Dr. Babb had quite a business, and he handled it so discretely that no one ever suspected. He even had printed instructions to be followed by the persons who were going to get the children.

"Unfortunate young women who found themselves in trouble could go to Dr. Babb. He would arrange to place them in homes where they could work for their board and room until the last six weeks. Then they went to his private hospital and waited. When the child was born, the mother got a thousand dollars and knew that she would never see the child again. Dr. Babb promised her it would have a good home. That was all he would say.

"For most of the women that was enough. An unfortu-

47

nate girl could tell her friends she was going away to visit distant relatives. A few months later she could return with new clothes and a story of having had a swell job she finally quit because of being homesick.

"Dr. Babb was very, very clever. Very few of the girls even knew his name. He had another doctor, an assistant who ran the hospital where the babies were actually delivered."

"Know his name?"

"No."

"Go on."

"Well, in the meantime, the foster mother was waiting at the other hospital. She had been there for some ten days after having practiced an elaborate deception on her friends.

"Dr. Babb covered everything very carefully with his printed instructions. His service cost a lot of money. He wouldn't touch a case for under ten thousand dollars."

Mason regarded Norma Logan thoughtfully. "You knew that Dr. Babb was dead?" he asked.

"Yes."

"Before I told you?"

"Yes."

"Who told you?"

"Mr. Kirby."

"When?"

"When he phoned a short time ago."

"Look," Mason told her, "I am representing the guy. I've got to find him. I've got to find him immediately. Seconds are precious. He didn't go near his office all afternoon. His house phone doesn't answer. Now where can I reach him?"

She shook her head. "I can't help you on that. He . . . he's keeping out of sight."

"Why?"

"So the situation will crystallize before he's called on to face the police."

Mason started pacing the floor. Abruptly he whirled once

more to face Norma Logan. "All right. Let's hear about Ronnie, and how you came to know John Kirby, and what really happened last night."

"My father," she said, "was one of the most wonderful men in the world. He was an adventurer, impractical, but dashing and magnetic.

"I hardly remember my mother at all. After she died, I was my daddy's girl. We had wonderful times together. Sometimes he was in the chips and we'd travel, and sometimes he was broke and we'd get by on nothing.

"Then about eight years ago, Dad married again. About a year after the marriage he was completely wiped out. He trusted a partner who took him to the cleaners good and proper. Dad simply couldn't understand that. He was getting older and he couldn't understand that either. He still had the same spirit of romantic daring and adventure, but—well, he wasn't young any more.

"He went on an expedition to South America, up in the jungles. That expedition was going to make him rich again. After a few weeks we received a report he had died. He left his second wife pregnant, and penniless. I was a green seventeen-year-old kid who knew a little shorthand, and I tried to stand by. I promised my stepmother that I'd get a job and support her. What a laugh that was: I couldn't do more than provide myself with the bare essentials.

"My stepmother heard of Dr. Babb's so-called service. And so I had a half-brother whom I never saw. My stepmother died a few months later, brokenhearted and disillusioned. She was terribly in love with my father up to the day she died. Dad had that way about him. When women fell in love with him, they just never got over it. I think they all recognized his shortcomings, but his fascination, his charm, and his gallantry, his romantic way of looking at life made him a perpetual prince charming.

"I had the name of Dr. Babb. I knew Ronnie had been placed somewhere. I couldn't find any records, however.

Then a short time ago, while putting together the few facts I had, I suddenly realized how Dr. Babb must have worked the whole thing. So I went back and consulted the records. I knew Ronnie's birthday. I looked up the birth records as of that day, and then looked up each birth certificate. As it happened it was a day when there was only one birth certificate signed by Dr. Babb. That was the birth of a son to John and Joan Kirby.

"For a while, I thought I'd try and look up the Kirbys without letting them know who I was just so I could get a look at my half-brother. I felt certain he'd look like Dad. If he does, if he has the fine, magnetic charm, that devil-may-care gallantry, the world will be his oyster. I was terribly anxious to look him up. Then I thought I hadn't better."

"What *did* you do?" Mason asked.

"I went to Dr. Babb," she said. "I told him who I was and what I wanted."

"What did you want?"

"I wanted to be assured that Ronnie was happy and was in a good home."

"And what happened?"

"Dr. Babb was terribly upset that I'd found him, but when I explained how I felt, he was greatly relieved. It seems this doctor who was his assistant had fallen on evil ways. He was a narcotic addict and he wanted money.

"When Dr. Babb knew I'd found out about Ronnie by investigative work he was very co-operative. He assured me Ronnie was very happy. He promised that he would get in touch with me if at any time he felt there was anything that was going to interfere with Ronnie's happiness. On the strength of that assurance, I decided that I'd just keep in the background and not try to see Ronnie or get acquainted."

"And then?" Mason asked.

"Then last Friday Dr. Babb telephoned. He said that I wasn't to get alarmed but that someone was trying to blackmail him. He said someone had found out what had been going on in the Kirby case, but lacked the definite evidence."

"Now, wait a minute," Mason said. "Did he say 'in the Kirby case' or was it in all his cases, and that he was calling you because of your interest in the Kirby case?"

"No, he said it was somebody who was only interested in the Kirby case."

"All right. What did you do?"

"I went out and saw him, and then yesterday afternoon I telephoned John Kirby at his office. I told him I had to see him on a matter of the greatest importance, that it had something to do with the welfare of his son."

"What happened?"

"I couldn't get Kirby until afternoon. He was very much disturbed. He told me that he was having a sales meeting at a roadhouse called the Purple Swan, that he would be tied up until after eleven o'clock, but that if I'd meet him there at eleven o'clock, he'd be very glad to see me."

"You met him there?"

"Yes."

"And then what?"

"I told him what had happened. We decided to go and see Dr. Babb."

"You telephoned Dr. Babb?"

"No."

"What did you do?"

"We just drove by the place, and saw that there was a light on in the house. Mr. Kirby felt that it would be better for me to go first and find out if the coast was clear. He was afraid that someone else might be there, and he didn't want any other person to see him in that house. He said that no one could *prove* anything, and for that reason, he wasn't going to have any personal contact with Dr. Babb that anyone could establish."

"So what did you do?"

"Mr. Kirby parked his car on one of the side streets. I

51

got out and went to the house. I started to ring the bell, and then decided to try the front door, the one which led into the reception room. It was unlocked. I opened the door and went on in."

"And then?" Mason asked.

"I'm going to tell you the truth now, Mr. Mason."

"That's what I want."

"Well, I sat down and within a short time, I guess less than a minute, I heard this terrific commotion from one of the inner rooms. There must have been a struggle going on. I could hear trampling feet and I thought I heard a blow and I distinctly heard a thud. Something that jarred the entire house. And then I heard a woman screaming."

"You *heard* a woman screaming?" Mason exclaimed.

"That's right."

"You didn't scream yourself?"

She shook her head.

"What did you do?" Mason asked.

"I ran to the door."

"The front door?"

"No, no! The door to the inner office where the commotion was taking place."

"What happened?"

"I opened that door and a body—I suppose it was that of Dr. Babb—was lying on the floor. A woman who had her back to me was standing over him, bending down."

"Did you ever see her face?"

"Yes, as she straightened I had a look at her profile."

"Can you describe her?"

"She was somewhere in the early thirties. She was well groomed, had a slightly upturned nose, dark hair and eyebrows, a mature sort of woman, but not heavy, not fat."

"Then what happened?"

"She ran toward the back of the house."

"And then?" Mason asked.

She said, "Mr. Mason, I did something that probably I

shouldn't have done, but if I had it to do over again, I'd do it."

"What?"

"I stole Dr. Babb's confidential records."

"What do you mean, his confidential records?"

"The only one that he kept, the only master book that showed where his babies had gone."

"How did you know he had it?"

"I spied on him, Mr. Mason. He looked up some information about Ronnie, about his birthday and so forth, and—well, he thought I was in the reception room. Actually I had gone into one of the dressing rooms and had the door open a crack. I was peeping out because I wanted to know where he kept this information I knew he was going to look up.

"Dr. Babb was pretty smart. He kept most of his records in nicely bound, expensive books, but there was one book in a cheap, pasteboard cover with a spiral binding that didn't look like anything particularly important and that was the one he looked at when he was finding out about Ronnie. He didn't even keep that book in the safe. He kept it in a little secret drawer in his desk."

"What did you do?"

"When I saw this woman, I was satisfied she was after this record because his safe door was open and books and documents had been tumbled out on the floor. I felt certain that when she dashed out the back door, she had probably taken *some* book with her that she *thought* was the record book she wanted. I knew that the police would come and—well, I knew that if this record book ever fell into the hands of the police there'd be the devil to pay. I was thinking not only of Ronnie but of all the other children who were like Ronnie.

"You can understand what it means, Mr. Mason, when a child had been raised to think he's in the security of a home with natural parents and then suddenly finds out that he's

53

an adopted child, and—And then of course there's the question of what the authorities would do. Here are heaven knows how many children with birth certificates that aren't worth the paper they're written on. And if anyone actually had the true facts—Of course, the difficulty would be in getting the true facts. But with the master records to go by, detectives could trace down those facts, and—well, you can see what would happen."

"So you got this book?" Mason prompted.

"I got it, Mr. Mason. I stuck it down my dress and ran out of that house just as fast as I could go. I knew that there had been enough commotion so that the neighbors would call the police. I felt there was nothing I could do for Dr. Babb and nothing I could do by staying there and being found there."

"Just what did you do?"

"I ran back to Mr. Kirby's car. I told him that I had to get to a place of concealment fast. I saw the woman who lives up on the hill above Dr. Babb's house standing in the doorway of her house as I ran out. The porch light was on at Dr. Babb's house and I'm satisfied she had a good look at me."

"So what happened?"

"Mr. Kirby started driving away from there. A police car went tearing past us before we'd gone half a block. I told Mr. Kirby we might run into a roadblock. No one was looking for a man, but they might very well be looking for a woman of my description."

"So you decided to stop at a motel?" Mason asked.

"We didn't then, but as we drove along we saw this motel with a sign saying, 'Vacancy,' and Mr. Kirby ran the car in there. I told him to register as husband and wife. That was the only way we could have any safety and get a unit. So he registered as husband and wife and we moved in. After a few minutes Mr. Kirby drove away by himself."

"Then what?"

"Then he returned about four or five o'clock in the morning, picked me up, drove me back to the Purple Swan where I'd left my car, and I got in it and drove home."

"And he told you what to say in case you were questioned?"

"Yes, then and later. He said I was to tell that story about the automobile and having run out of gas, but he said no one would ever question me because they couldn't ever find out who I was. He said that if the going should get tough and *he* had to bolster up *his* story, he'd suddenly remember something about me that would enable detectives to locate me at this address, and then I could substantiate his story."

"Did you tell him about the book?" Mason asked.

She said, "I've told no one about the book."

"Where is it?" Mason asked.

"I have it."

Mason shook his head. "I've found you. Police can find you. This isn't an assault any more. It's a murder case. You're going to be charged with murder."

"*I* am?" she asked incredulously.

"Sure. What the hell did you think?"

"But Mr. Mason, the woman who killed him was the one who screamed, the one who was in the inside office."

"Look," Mason told her. "Don't be naïve. You went to Dr. Babb's house. You were concerned about the security of Ronson Kirby. At least that's *your* story. As far as the police are concerned, they may feel that you were hired by John Kirby to go get that book. I don't know. I have your word for it, that's all.

"*You* say that there was another woman in there, a woman who screamed."

"Well, that's what happened. The neighbors heard her scream."

"The neighbors heard a woman scream," Mason said, "but the police will act on the assumption that you went

55

there for the definite purpose of stealing this book, that Dr. Babb had left the front door open, that you entered the reception room and opened the door to the inner office. Dr. Babb was probably in another part of the house. You saw your opportunity. You slipped in and tried to steal this book. Dr. Babb came in and caught you at it. There was a struggle. You cracked him over the head with a beaker, probably only intending to knock him out or keep him from grabbing you. But you hit him too hard. That's when you screamed. Then you grabbed the book and ran out."

"But, Mr. Mason, I'm telling you the truth. There *was* another woman in there."

"Perhaps there was. But *you're* lying to me."

"What do you mean?"

"You said that you and Kirby went to see Dr. Babb cold turkey, that you didn't telephone or have any appointment."

"We didn't."

"Then," Mason said, "how does it happen that Dr. Babb's appointment book showed that he had a late evening appointment with both of you? Your names are both in his book."

She looked at Mason with wide, startled eyes. "Did Kirby telephone him?" Mason asked.

"He . . . he must have."

"All right," Mason told her. "You're hotter than a stove lid as far as the police are concerned. I found you and they're going to find you. Give me that notebook and then get out of here."

"Where shall I go?"

"That's up to you," Mason said. "But for a while at least don't be where the police can pick you up.

"And I'll tell you something else because it's my duty to tell you as a lawyer. If you get out of here, that can be evidence against you. It can be evidence of flight, but I'll give you one ray of hope. I happen to know that there *was* another woman in the house and I'm going to try my damnedest to find out who she was. I don't have a single solitary thing to work on right now except perhaps a question of fingerprints which the police may uncover."

"How much time do I have?" she asked.

Mason shrugged his shoulders. "Perhaps two seconds. Perhaps two weeks. If Kirby phones again, tell him to ring the Drake Detective Agency in my building and leave word where I can reach him. Tell him the message will be relayed to me at any hour of the day or night, and tell him it's damned important."

"And you don't think I should tell that story he told me to?"

"I can't advise you. I can only tell you to get a lawyer of your own, and do it at once. In the meantime, I want that book."

"Why?"

"To make certain it doesn't get into the hands of the police or into the hands of a blackmailer."

"I can't give it to you."

"Why?"

"I . . . I don't know. I trust you, but I *know* it's safe with me."

"No, it isn't," Mason said. "You're hotter than a firecracker. You're going to be picked up. Police will search you and go through your car."

She looked at him a moment, then turned to Della Street. "Will you come with me a moment, Miss Street? I want to talk with you, woman to woman."

Della Street flashed a swift glance at Mason, then said, "All right. Where do you want me to go?"

Norma Logan opened the bathroom door. She and Della went inside. The door was locked. After a few moments, the lock clicked back and the door opened.

Norma Logan said, "I'm not going to give it to you, Mr. Mason. You are in a way just as hot as I am. I've talked

57

with Miss Street. We've thought of a safe place for that book."

Mason glanced at Della. She met his eyes, gave a brief nod of her head.

"Have you told Kirby anything about this book?" Mason asked.

She shook her head. "I didn't know how far I could trust Mr. Kirby."

"All right," Mason said. "Don't tell him. Don't tell anybody."

"If I should be questioned by the police, should I tell them the story Mr. Kirby told me to tell?"

"There," Mason said, "I'm not in a position to advise you. Understand definitely that I'm not your lawyer. I'm representing John Kirby. I'd suggest that you consult a lawyer *at once*, that you tell him what happened, and that you take his advice. I'm on my way. Come on, Della."

Della Street waited until they were in the automobile leaving the Mananas Apartments.

"May I ask a question, Chief?" she said at length.

"Sure, go ahead."

"That woman isn't your client?"

"Definitely not."

"Yet you asked her for that notebook."

"Yes."

"Why?"

"Because," Mason said, "from what she told me I knew that that notebook was too dangerous to leave kicking around. In the first place, I'm representing John Kirby. I realize now what was bothering him when he came in to see me this afternoon. I'm trying to protect his son."

"Is it ethical?" Della Street answered.

"Hell, no!" Mason said, "it isn't ethical. That notebook is stolen property, Della. If I take it into my possession, I become an accessory after the fact. I'd be violating the Penal Code. I'd have possession of stolen property, and I haven't the faintest intention of letting that property get to the police."

"And if I should have that book, where would it leave you professionally?"

"Behind the eight ball if I *knew* you had it."

He drove for a while in silence, then said somewhat savagely, "Ethics are rules of conduct that are made to preserve the dignity and the integrity of the profession. I'm inclined to conform to the spirit of the rules of ethics rather than the letter."

"But what about the courts?"

"They'll conform to the letter rather than the spirit. If the police ever find out that girl had that notebook and that it came under my control, and that information should get to Hamilton Burger, the district attorney, who hates the very ground I walk on, he'll have the opportunity he's been waiting for. He'll charge me with receiving stolen property. He'll throw the Penal Code at me."

"And then what will *you* do?"

"Then," Mason said, "I'll truthfully say that I don't *know* where the book is. I know one thing, Della, I'm not going to rip the veil off the past, and throw heaven knows how many children to the wolves.

"That's the worst of the law. It has to conform to the letter. It can't cut corners. If the law finds out that these children were illegally placed in homes, the law will *have* to declare them the wards of the state. Then the parents can only try to get the children by adoption proceedings. A lot of children who have had all the security of thinking that they are in their own natural home with their own natural parents will learn the truth. The case will get a lot of newspaper publicity, some of the mothers will come forward, blackmailers will move in, there'll be hell to pay."

"And *you're* willing to risk your reputation and *your* liberty to keep that from happening?"

Mason grinned at her. "You're darned right I am. I'm a

59

lawyer. It may sound corny, but my life is dedicated to improving the administration of justice. I'm loyal to my clients. I'm trying to represent John Kirby and his son. But don't start hanging any crepe on the office door as yet. I have a certain amount of human ingenuity, considerable legal agility, and I'm going to use them both.

"And," he added, after a moment, "I don't *know* where the book is now."

"What about Kirby?" Della Street asked. "Are you going to try to find him?"

"How can I? He's gone to cover at least for the moment. It was a fool thing to do, but he's done it. If he gets in touch with Norma Logan, she'll deliver my message that he's to call Paul Drake. Drake will see that he gets in touch with me. I'll tell Drake to have an operative watch Kirby's house and tell Kirby to call me if he or his wife returns home. I'll meet Paul Drake at seven-forty-five tomorrow morning in case I don't hear from Kirby before that. There's no use for us to sit up and beat our brains out. We'll need a night's sleep. Tomorrow's pretty apt to be one hell of a day."

"You can say that again," Della Street murmured.

Chapter 6

Seven-forty-five o'clock in the morning found Perry Mason at Paul Drake's office. The detective was a few minutes late.

"Hi, Perry," Paul said. "What's the great idea?"

"Trying to do an honest day's work," Mason said grinning. "What's the idea of being ten minutes late?"

Drake looked at his watch. "It's only eight and a half minutes. I've been digging out material."

"What?"

"I've been putting two and two together."

"How come?" Mason asked.

Drake settled himself in the creaking swivel chair behind the battered desk. Tall, dull-eyed, unemotional, he had carefully studied the art of blending into his environment and flattening himself into insignificance.

"On that Dr. Babb case," he said. "Police got a good description of a young woman who ran out the front door of that house."

Mason lit a cigarette.

"They wondered how it happened the girl was able to disappear so completely, because the police were on the job almost within a matter of seconds. They called other police cars, and threw out a pretty good net."

"A girl can go a long ways in a short time in an automobile," Mason said.

"*Provided* she has the automobile," Drake said, "and *provided* it's parked reasonably near to the scene of operations. In this particular instance police are working on the theory that the girl was on foot."

"Go ahead," Mason said.

"In which event," Drake said, "she must have got off the streets in a hurry. So just as a matter of routine, the police started checking a motel that was in the neighborhood, the Beauty Rest Motel."

"Find anything?" Mason asked noncommittally.

"Not what they were looking for at the time, but they found something that ties in."

"What?"

"They were asking if some young, unattached woman, answering a certain description, had registered in the motel at about eleven-forty to eleven-forty-five Monday evening. They were asking about unescorted women.

"The manager told them that, while there had been no unescorted young women of that description, a couple had registered at the time mentioned, under rather suspicious circumstances. They had registered as husband and wife. The so-called husband, however, had left the motel, leaving the woman there alone, and the time of his departure was such that the manager became a little suspicious. He said the man wasn't in the unit more than a few minutes."

"Uh-huh," Mason said.

"When the police checked the room where Dr. Babb had been assaulted, they naturally dusted for fingerprints. They didn't find any fingerprints on the glass beaker that had been used as a weapon, but they *did* find some fingerprints that weren't those of Dr. Babb or of his handy man. From the manner in which one of the fingerprints had been superimposed on a print which the police felt certain had been made by Dr. Babb a short time before the assault, police had the idea they might have the fingerprint of the assailant."

"So what did they do?"

"Went to Unit 5 in the Beauty Rest Motel," Drake said,

"and took fingerprints. They got the fingerprints of this same woman."

"That makes it interesting, doesn't it?" Mason said.

"Very," Drake said.

"Now then, the police picked up Dr. Babb's appointment book. It showed he had three or four appointments for the afternoon, and two for the evening. They were listed as Kirby and Logan."

"No first names or initials?"

"No first names or initials," Drake said.

"Go on," Mason told him. "Anything else?"

"So naturally," Drake said, "the police became very much interested in the identity of the man who had driven this young woman to the Beauty Rest Motel. He had registered under a name which proved to be phony and an address which was fictitious, but he had given the make and license number of his automobile.

"That license number also turned out to be phony, but apparently it's phony only as to two numbers. The manager of the motel *thought* he had checked the number given on the registration card with the license number of the automobile. He says that he knows that he checked the first three letters which are JYJ. The next digit is listed on the registration card as a one and the manager feels certain that it was a one. The discrepancy in the license number, therefore, must lie with the last two digits, and that narrows the search to ninety-nine cars. Since the police know the make of the car they are looking for, it's going to take them only a very short time to get the data they want."

"Uh-huh," Mason observed.

"So," Drake told him, "knowing that you're very anxious to get in touch with Kirby, knowing that the name Kirby was on Dr. Babb's appointment book—well, I've been putting two and two together. That's all."

"Find out anything?" Mason asked.

"Not yet. No one has shown up at the Kirby residence.

It was dark all night. The garage doors are closed and locked. Of course, Perry, if the police should pick up Kirby and if they should find the fingerprints of this young woman in Kirby's car, it would quite naturally put Kirby in one hell of a spot. He'd have to tell who the young woman was. He'd have to explain why he registered the way he did. In view of the fact that the case is now a murder—well, there'd be hell to pay."

"And you think that police are hot on the trail?" Mason asked.

"You bet they're hot on the trail," Drake said. "They'll—"

He broke off as a telephone rang shrilly. "Here it starts," Drake said grinning. "The life of a detective. Glamorous in fiction, but for the most part sitting at the end of a telephone correlating information. Stick around, Perry."

Drake picked up the receiver, said, "Hello. . . . Yeah, this is Drake. . . . Oh-oh, where are you? Okay, hold on for instructions."

Drake turned to Perry Mason. "That's my operative out at the Kirby house," he said. "The Kirbys showed up about ten minutes ago. My man had to drive down to a service station to telephone. He wants to know whether you want him to go back and keep the place under surveillance, or—"

"Tell him to come on in," Mason said, "and not to hang around the house. If there's any chance police may show up, I don't want them to collar your man and shake him down to find out what he's doing there."

"Okay," Drake said. He turned to the telephone and said, "Come on in, Bill. . . . Yeah, that's right. To the office."

Drake hung up.

Mason reached for the phone, said to Drake's switchboard operator, "I want the residence of John Kirby. I want to talk with Kirby personally. The number is Bayside 9–6 something or other. I'm not sure of the last three numbers. Get him for me, will you? Okay, I'll hold the line."

Mason waited on the line, and after some thirty seconds heard the voice of Drake's telephone operator, "Mr. Kirby is on the line, Mr. Mason."

Mason said, "Okay, thanks." The line clicked.

"Hello," Kirby said.

"This is Perry Mason, Kirby," the lawyer said.

"Oh yes, Mason."

"Where the hell have you been?" Mason asked.

"What do you mean, where the hell have I been?" Kirby asked indignantly. "I've been out on a short business trip. I had my wife and son with me. Why? What's it all about?"

Mason said, "It's too long to tell you over the phone and too dangerous. You wait there for me. I'm coming out. Under no circumstances leave the place until I arrive."

"But what in the world are you—?"

"There isn't any time to explain," Mason said, "and don't act so damned innocent."

Mason slammed up the phone. "I'm on my way, Paul," he said. "No, wait a minute. Let me call Della."

Mason held onto the telephone, clicked the connection, said to Drake's exchange operator, "How about getting Della Street for me? You have her number."

"Right away, Mr. Mason," she said.

A moment later Della Street's voice came over the phone.

"Had breakfast?" Mason asked.

"Just leaving for the office," she answered.

"Stick around," Mason told her. "I'm going out to Kirby's. I'll drive by your apartment and pick you up. You have notebooks and pencils?"

"Uh-huh, I'll be waiting down in front with my brief case all loaded. I'll be there in exactly ten minutes and wait until you come."

"Good girl!" Mason told her.

Mason hung up, said to Drake, "Your operator has the number of Kirby's residence. Call me out there if anything vitally important happens. Otherwise, wait until I call you. I should be back in my office by ten o'clock."

Mason hurried to the elevator, picked up his car in the parking lot, and drove past the building where Della Street had her apartment exactly twelve minutes from the time he had left Drake's office. Della Street was standing by the curb, trim and efficient, a leather brief case held in her gloved hand.

Mason slid the car to a stop, held the door open.

"What's new, Chief?" she asked.

"Quite a bit," Mason said. "You're looking fine this morning."

"Thanks."

"It's a real pleasure to have someone like you, Della. I wish I could tell you what it means."

"You can't?" she asked swinging her legs into the car and slamming the door shut.

"Not in words."

"Well, you can always try," she said smiling. "Ears are very receptive to words of that sort, no matter how inadequate they may be."

Mason grinned. "All right," he said. "It's nice to have you around. It's nice to know that I can trust you in a pinch, that you know me well enough to know exactly what I want you to do in any given set of circumstances. It's nice to have your loyalty, your dependability, and . . . and you're easy on the eyes."

"Well," she said, "*those* words weren't very inadequate. Thanks, Chief."

Mason was silent for a moment, then said, "Kirby was out all last night. Apparently on a business trip. I would be more inclined to be credulous and considerate if we didn't know that he'd called Norma Logan."

"I take it that, when we meet Mr. Kirby this time," Della

Street said, "he is going to hear a little lecture about the fallacy of lying to his lawyer."

"If we have time," Mason said, "we're *really* going to rake that bird over the coals."

"And then what?"

"Then," Mason said, "I want to find out whether I'm representing him as his lawyer. After all, he only came to the office to tell me a story and that's the last opportunity I've had to check with him. Everything else I've done on my own. I'm putting in a lot of time, and running up quite a bill for detectives."

"Wouldn't it have been better to have waited until you were sure?" she said.

"From a dollars and cents basis, yes," Mason said, "but somehow, Della, I'm not built that way. I want to protect a client and, knowing that while I was sitting around twiddling my thumbs waiting for a formal notice of employment and a retainer the case might have been blown wide open, I preferred to take a gamble."

"Part of the service you give clients," Della said.

"Part of the service I *try* to give clients," Mason told her. "Of course, you lose out sometimes, but in the long run it winds up on the credit side of the ledger."

Again they drove in silence until Mason said, "That street is right along here someplace, Della. Take a look at the names on the street signs, will you? Oh-oh, here it is right here."

Mason made a right-hand turn and drove for three blocks.

"That'll be the house over there on the left, Della."

"*Some* house!" she said.

Mason said, "I presume Mr. John Kirby has done right well for himself. We'll soon find out a little more about Mr. John Kirby and a *lot* more about the case."

Mason parked the car in front of the house and he and

Della Street hurried up the long strip of cement sidewalk which led to the front porch.

Mason pushed his thumb against the mother-of-pearl bell button. They heard chimes in the interior of the house but no sounds of activity from within.

Mason frowned, looked at his watch. "Hang it," he said, "seconds are precious and they fool around answering the door."

"Do they know you're coming?" Della asked.

"Yes, I told Kirby to be here and—" Mason jabbed savagely at the button, ringing the chimes in steady sequence.

"Well," Della Street said at length, "it doesn't seem to be just a question of waiting to answer the bell. It would seem to be there's no one home."

Mason said, "If he took it on himself to take a powder—"

"What about Mrs. Kirby?"

"I didn't talk with her personally," Mason said, "but she's home. The three of them were away all night. They showed up half an hour ago."

"Who's the third?"

"Ronson."

"Oh yes. They'd all been away together?"

"That's right."

"So what do we do?" Della Street asked. "Just wait or go back to the office?"

"I don't want to do either," Mason told her. "If we go back to the office, we'll lose valuable time. I want to get in touch with Kirby. He wants me to realize that he's a big executive and can do his own thinking. He thinks I know nothing whatever about Dr. Babb and that I'm hounding him for more details about that story he told us of picking up the hitchhiker on the highway. Let's take a look in the garage, Della."

Mason left the porch, led the way around across the lawn to the three-car garage. He tried one of the doors and found it securely locked. The next door was locked and so was the third.

"Well," Mason said, "I guess we'd better wait until someone shows up. Let's go sit in the car and wait at least a few minutes, Della."

They started walking back down the driveway. Suddenly Mason turned at a noise behind him.

The garage doors had swung upward, and the interior of the garage showed one vacant stall, two stalls with cars parked in them.

"What in the world?" Della Street gasped. "How did those doors open?"

Mason whirled, "Come on, Della," he said, and started walking rapidly toward the garage.

"What is it?" she asked. "Did someone see us there and—"

"A ray of black light," Mason said. "It's fixed so that, when they swing one of their cars in the driveway, the garage doors all open. Probably they stay open for a matter of sixty seconds or something of that sort and then close."

"But, Chief," Della Street said, "doesn't that make the garage vulnerable to any prowler or—?"

"They can undoubtedly turn a switch on the inside of the house and shut this mechanism off," Mason told her. "The fact that it's been left on indicates they intend to be back within a short time. Probably Kirby wanted to go somewhere and felt he could get back before I arrived. Come on, Della. Let's go in before the doors close."

They entered the garage and Mason started looking around.

"Now this big Olds with the license plate JYJ 112 is undoubtedly the car Kirby was driving night before last," Mason said. "Then they have a sports car over there, and the vacant stall is where—" He broke off as the three doors of the garage swung silently downward and clicked into place.

"Evidently," Mason said, "we trip another timing mechanism as we go through the door of the garage."

"And now we're locked in?" Della Street asked.

Mason looked around the garage and said, "No, that door leads to the house. Let's see if it's unlocked."

Della Street, who was nearer to the door, turned the knob. "It's unlocked," she said. She opened it and said, "It opens into a passageway which seems to go right into the house."

"All right," Mason told her. "I'm interested in this car Kirby was driving last night. Let's take a look at it."

Mason looked at the outside of the car for a moment, then opened the door. "Oh-oh."

"What?" Della Street asked.

"A gallon can of gasoline," Mason said holding it up.

"Well, well, well," Della Street observed. "*Now* he has the props to back up his story."

Mason pressed his thumb against the catch of the glove compartment, opened it, looked inside and pulled out a small printed slip of paper, then began to chuckle.

"What is it?" Della Street asked.

"Our friend Kirby is unspeakably naïve," Mason said. "He not only bought this gasoline can from a service station but he got a sales slip with it and then forgot and left the sales slip in the glove compartment of his automobile."

"When's it dated?" Della Street asked.

"It's dated yesterday," Mason told her. "He probably went out right after his interview with me and purchased an authentic, slightly battered, red gasoline can."

"What are you going to do?"

"I'll just put this sales slip in my pocket. I'll leave the gasoline can where it is. Then later on when Kirby tells us, all smiles, that the gasoline can was in his automobile all the time but was down back of the front seat and he just hadn't noticed it, I'll ask him what became of the *other* gasoline can, and he'll want to know, of course with a show of indignation, what other gasoline can I'm talking about, and then I'll flash this sales slip on him and say, 'The one you bought yesterday at the Chevron station at Figueroa and Atcheson streets, of course.' "

"He'll wonder how you found out about it," Della Street said.

"Let him," Mason told her. "It won't do him any harm to do a little speculating."

Della Street thoughtfully regarded the automobile. "Do you suppose he'll think his wife is mixed up in it, that she went through the glove compartment, and—"

"That's right," Mason said. "You have a point there, Della. I'll have to—" He broke off in midsentence at the sound of a metallic click. Without other warning, the three doors of the garage swung upward, disclosing a dark blue sedan in the driveway.

A good-looking young woman at the wheel of the sedan piloted it expertly through the open doors of the garage, opened the car door and slid part way out before she noticed Perry Mason and Della Street.

With an exclamation of embarrassed surprise, she grabbed at her skirt which had been dragging behind her on the seat, whipped it down and said, "Who are you, and what are *you* doing in *here*?"

The mechanism sent the garage doors swinging silently downward.

"Permit me to introduce myself. I'm Perry Mason."

"*You* are!"

"Yes. You're Mrs. Kirby?"

"Yes."

"This is Miss Street, my confidential secretary. We came out here to talk with your husband, and minutes are precious."

"Well, why aren't you in the house talking with him?"

"Because," Mason said, "no one seems to answer the doorbell. We walked around to see if the garage might be open. It wasn't. Then we walked back toward my car, which is parked in front, intending to wait there, and the garage doors obligingly flew open."

She suddenly laughed. The sharp edge of irritation left her voice. "Well, at least our garage was hospitable if my husband wasn't," she said.

"I'm afraid he isn't home," Mason said.

"Oh yes, he is. His car's here. He told me you'd phoned that you were on your way out and that he was waiting for you. I left to take Ronnie to school."

"Your husband didn't answer the doorbell," Mason said.

"He may have been in the bathroom. We'll go dig him out. Why are you out here, Mr. Mason? Has there been some development?"

"There are lots of developments," the lawyer said grimly. "I tried to get you people on the telephone all yesterday afternoon and evening."

"We went with John on a business trip. Is it anything serious?"

"Very serious. You can listen in when I talk with your husband, Mrs. Kirby."

"That's fine," she told him. "We'll get him. Come on in."

She opened the door from the garage into the passageway which led to a reception hallway in the house.

"Only your husband home?" Mason asked.

"It's the servants' day off," she explained. "We keep a cook and a housekeeper, and I let them both off on the same day. Wednesdays John and I usually dine out and Ronnie spends the afternoon and evening with a young friend. They take care of Ronnie during Wednesday when our servants are off and we take care of their youngster Thursdays when their servants are off. It makes a very nice arrangement. Come on in and sit down. I'll get John for you."

72

She indicated seats in a spacious living room and called, "John! Oh, John!"

There was no answer.

"Sit down and be comfortable, folks," she invited, "or look around. John is undoubtedly upstairs. He may be in the shower. I'll find him."

Abruptly lowering her voice she said to Mason, "John's story about that girl in the jacket with the mother-of-pearl buttons, the alligator shoes, do you believe there really was such a girl?"

"Yes," Mason said.

Her face showed surprise. "You believe his story, then, about—?"

"No," Mason interrupted, "I don't believe his story. I have to get to him and tip him off to certain things about that story. Will you get him, please?"

"Right away," she promised. "He's upstairs somewhere."

She ran up the stairs and Mason walked across to the bookcases and inspected the volumes. Della Street looked at some of the paintings, then settled herself in a chair.

From time to time they heard steps upstairs, and twice they heard Mrs. Kirby calling her husband.

At length she came downstairs. "Mr. Mason, I'm afraid something's gone wrong somewhere."

"Why?" Mason asked.

"John isn't here."

"Where would he have gone?"

"No place. His car's in the garage."

"You've looked the place over?" Mason asked sharply.

"I've looked the place over—that is, I looked in all the bathrooms and bedrooms and every place I could think of, and I've called. Of course," she said, her face suddenly white and strained, "I didn't look in the closets."

"Your husband may have been taken away against his will, or he may have decided he was up against something he didn't want to face. Look in the closets."

She took one quick look at his face, then flew upstairs.

"We'll look around downstairs," Mason called up to her.

Mason and Della Street looked through the dining room, the downstairs bedrooms, the maids' rooms, the basement, the pantry, opening closet doors, giving the place a thorough search. When they returned, Mrs. Kirby was in the living room.

"He simply isn't in the house," she said.

"All right," Mason told her. "There's only one answer to that."

"What?"

"He was taken away."

"What do you mean?"

"By the police."

She looked at him with wide, startled eyes. "Mr. Mason, what in the world *are* you talking about?"

"There isn't any time to tell you now," Mason said. "I want you to answer two or three questions and answer them fast. If the police question your husband, will he tell them the same story that he told me yesterday afternoon?"

"I suppose so. I know that you jarred his self-complacency when you pointed out certain discrepancies in that story, but—well, you have to understand John's character to understand his reactions. He'd try to bolster up the weak points in the story, and . . . I know he intended to see you again today and he felt that he could convince you of the truth of what he had told you yesterday."

Mason said, "If the police should start tripping him up, would he have sense enough to tell them he wasn't going to answer any more questions until he had talked with me, or would he go ahead and try to explain?"

"I'm afraid he'd try to explain, Mr. Mason. You see he's been a salesman all his life. He's accustomed to meeting the objections of a prospect and explaining them away. If the police give him a chance he'll talk and keep talking."

"That's what I was afraid of," Mason said. "Come on, Della."

"Where are you going?" she asked.

Mason said, "In view of your husband's prominence, I don't think they'll book him right away. I think they'll take him to the district attorney's office. That's where I'm going."

"But why in the world should they take him to the district attorney's office?" Mrs. Kirby asked. "What on earth are they going to question him about?"

Mason and Della Street started for the door. "Murder," Mason called back over his shoulder.

Chapter 7

Mason piloted his car through traffic, conscious of the fact that the police already had a head start which was lengthening with each delay.

By the time Mason reached the district attorney's office, it was after nine-thirty.

"Is Mr. Hamilton Burger, the district attorney, in?" Mason asked.

"Yes."

"Tell him Perry Mason wishes to see him, please."

"I'm sorry. Mr. Burger left word that he isn't to be disturbed under any circumstances. I'm not permitted to call him on the phone or to interrupt in any way. He's in a very important conference."

Mason said, "I have a client in here."

"Who?" she asked.

"Mr. John Northrup Kirby. I demand to see him at once."

"You will have to ask Mr. Burger about that."

"Then tell him I'm here."

"I can't. He's not to be disturbed."

Mason said, "He's talking with John Kirby. I'm Kirby's counsel. I demand that I be permitted to see Mr. Kirby."

"I have no authority in the matter."

"You're in charge here, aren't you?"

"I'm only an employee."

"Then try to have me thrown out," Mason said, pushing past the woman's desk through a swinging door and down a long corridor toward Hamilton Burger's private office.

A startled deputy, evidently alerted by telephone, flung

open a door, debouched into the corridor. "You can't come in here," he said.

"I'm in here," Mason told him.

The deputy hurried to the lawyer's side.

"Get out."

"Put me out."

The deputy hesitated. Mason pushed his way to the door of Hamilton Burger's office, tried the knob. The door was locked. Mason banged his fist against the panels of the door.

Hamilton Burger's voice could be heard from the interior of the office. He was evidently talking on the phone and his voice was sharp with irritation.

Mason again banged his fist on the panels.

Abruptly the door was thrown open and Hamilton Burger, the big, grizzly bear of a district attorney who made no secret of his dislike for Perry Mason, stood glowering in the doorway.

"Don't bang on my door," he shouted. "I'll have you arrested."

"Go ahead," Mason invited. "I'm here to protect the rights of my client."

"And who's your client?"

"John Northrup Kirby," Mason said, raising his voice.

"Is he accused of crime?"

"I don't know," Mason said, "but he's my client. I'm here to protect his rights. I want to be present while he is being interviewed.'"

"We can't stand for that, Mason."

"Why not?" Mason asked.

"We're investigating a murder."

"Is Kirby implicated?"

"It's a little early to tell yet."

"Under those circumstances," Mason said, "the purpose of my request becomes even more apparent."

Mason looked at his wrist watch, noted the time and jotted that time down in a notebook. "I've made a formal demand on you," he said.

"Now wait a minute," Burger said, "you're not going to trap me with any technicality. Mr. Kirby, as far as I'm concerned, is merely a material witness, except of course the fact that he has retained a high-priced criminal attorney such as you indicates there's something in the background I don't know about."

"There can be lots of things in the background *you* don't know about," Mason said, "but the fact remains anyone has a right to retain me in connection with any matter he damn pleases, and I have a right to talk with my client."

"Your client was not brought here under process," Hamilton Burger said. "He came here voluntarily."

Mason kept his voice up. "Then he can leave here voluntarily. Come on, Kirby."

"We haven't finished questioning him," Burger said.

"I think you have," Mason said.

John Kirby came to stand behind Burger.

"I trust you realize," Burger said, "that any such attitude as this makes Mr. Kirby more of a suspect than a witness. I have been protecting him from all publicity in the case as a witness. As a suspect I can give him no such protection."

He turned to Kirby. "I trust you will appreciate the situation, Mr. Kirby. You have registered at a motel with a young woman as husband and wife. We have no desire to pillory you with publicity as long as you cooperate. I suggest you carefully consider the facts in the situation."

"Come on, Kirby, let's go!" Mason said.

"Can't this wait?" Kirby asked Mason. "Mr. Burger has been most considerate and—"

"Hell, no! It can't wait," Mason told him. "Get going if you want me to represent you."

Kirby hesitated.

"Make up your mind," Mason told him.

Kirby eased out into the hallway, his manner hesitant.

"All right, Mason," Burger said. "There's your client. Look him over. No bruises. No marks of a rubber hose. No torture. No pressure. No violence. How did we treat you, Kirby?"

"With every consideration," Kirby said.

Hamilton Burger grinned. "Your lawyer evidently doesn't have as much confidence in your story as you want us to have. He seems to feel that you need protection, that you need to be advised as to what he refers to as 'your rights.' "

Kirby's face flushed. "I didn't ask Mr. Mason to be here. I—"

"Never mind, Kirby," Mason said. "Don't let him lead you on. I'll explain to you in the car. Let's go!"

"Perhaps Kirby would like to have you explain right here and now," Hamilton Burger said. "Come in, Mason, and we'll talk things over. We may be able to get the whole matter cleared up."

"I'll talk to my client in private, if you don't mind," Mason said. "Come on, Kirby."

Hamilton Burger stood in the doorway grinning as Mason escorted his client to the elevator.

"What the devil!" Kirby said angrily. "That is the one touch I didn't want, Mason. Can't you understand the position in which you put me by busting in there? Good heavens, Mason! I'm not a child! I am a businessman. I'm accustomed to carrying on rather large and important business transactions, and if I do say so myself, I know my way around."

"I see," Mason said. "Perhaps you'd better wait and talk in the car."

Kirby drew himself up angrily. "I think I can talk any place I damn please, Mason. I'm trying to point out to you that, while I may call on you for advice as to the law, I don't need anyone to do my thinking for me."

"Exactly," Mason said. "You can tell me about it after we get in the car."

Kirby rode down in the elevator and strode alongside Mason to the parking place where Della Street was seated in the rear of the car.

"How do you do, Miss Street," he said gruffly.

"Get up in front," Mason told Kirby. "I'll drive you home."

"You don't need to," Kirby told him. "I can get a cab. It may be a lot cheaper in the long run, a hell of a lot cheaper. I don't know why you feel you have to chaperon me, Mason. I'm fully capable of taking care of myself."

"You told the district attorney about what happened Monday night?" Mason asked.

"Is there any reason why I shouldn't?"

"It's a hell of a story!" Mason said.

"I'm not accustomed to having my word doubted, Mr. Mason," Kirby said, getting into the car.

Mason started the motor.

"How did you know Dr. Babb had died?" Mason asked.

"Who's Dr. Babb?"

"The doctor you dealt with when you conspired to violate the laws in regard to adoption. The doctor whom you paid to list Ronson in the Vital Statistics as the son of you and your wife."

"I don't know what you're talking about," Kirby said sullenly.

"You may not know what I'm talking about now," Mason said, "but you sure as hell knew all about it last night when you called Norma Logan and told her Dr. Babb had died and instructed her to back up your story about having run out of gas on the highway, having her car stolen and abandoned by somebody out at the Purple Swan."

"Here again, I don't know what you're talking about," Kirby said. "The name Logan means nothing to me, and I certainly didn't ask anyone to back up my story. It is, of course, possible that you know something I don't, and that the young woman whom I picked up *did* have the name of Logan."

"You told that story to the district attorney?"

"Certainly."

"Just as you told it to me?"

"Yes. Why would I have changed it?"

"Well," Mason said, "that's done it. That puts the fat in the fire."

"What do you mean, the fat in the fire, Mason? Those people were courtesy itself. They were very, very considerate. They even refused to give out any tip to the newspapers so that I wouldn't be hounded by the press. They put it up to me that if I'd cooperate with them, they'd cooperate with me, and they're certainly doing a job!"

"Yes, I can imagine," Mason said, working his way through traffic and getting on the approach to the freeway.

"And, by the way," Kirby went on, "that gasoline can was in my car all the time, just as you surmised."

"I see," Mason said.

"I found it as soon as I went back to my car. However, I had this other appointment and I couldn't telephone you at the time, but I decided to let you know as soon as I could. And then the police showed up at my house and asked me if I'd mind having a talk with the district attorney about some information I seem to possess. How do they find out those things? I put down the first part of my license number correctly because I felt the manager would probably remember that, but the last two figures I juggled completely."

"Did you tell the officers about the gasoline can?"

"Certainly."

"About it being in your car?"

"Of course."

"Did they ask you to produce it?"

"They did better than that. A few minutes ago they put

81

out a call over the police radio and had a police car drive by the house and pick it up."

"Then probably they have it by this time," Mason said.

"And you don't need to be so stuffy about it," Kirby blazed.

"I just wanted to keep you in the clear," Mason said.

"Well, I'm in the clear," Kirby snapped. "You can trust my discretion in some things, Mr. Mason. I don't need you to hold my hand every time someone asks me a question."

Mason said, "I was afraid that you might give the officers permission to search your car and garage."

"Well, why not?" Kirby asked. "They would like very much to get fingerprints of this young woman, and there's no reason why I shouldn't help them. They already have her fingerprints from the unit in the motel. I don't know why they're so worked up about her. They wouldn't tell me that. They did ask me if I'd ever heard of a Dr. Babb."

"What did you tell them?"

"The truth. I don't think I ever heard of him in my life."

"You told the D.A. that?"

"Certainly."

"Said you'd never heard of him?"

"I said the name meant absolutely nothing to me. That's the truth, it doesn't. Now what's wrong with cooperating with the police in this thing? Why shouldn't I let them search my car if they want to? Why shouldn't I let them question and search to their heart's content?"

"Quite all right, if you feel that way," Mason told him. "Of course, when they search the car they'll dig into the glove compartment and look through any papers that might be there and—Well, when I heard you were at the D.A.'s office I just thought I'd better get in touch with you."

Kirby suddenly straightened up in the seat, his forehead puckered into a frown.

"What's the matter?" Mason asked.

"Nothing!" Kirby said shortly. "I . . . I was just thinking.

What'll they do about fingerprinting the car, Mason? Will they fingerprint it there in the garage?"

Mason said, "Probably they'll send a tow car around to pick up the front end and take it up to the police laboratory. I take it they asked you if you'd have any objection?"

"That's right."

"You told them you had no objection?"

"Of course. How long will it take them to get the tow car there?"

"Not very long."

"Hang it! Mason," Kirby said, "you're driving at a snail's pace! I've lost enough time over this thing as it is. I'd like to get home."

"Why?"

"Because I'm a busy man. You've been talking about that glove compartment. Come to think of it, there *may* be some business papers in there that I wouldn't want to have the public know about. I have competitors who would like to find out some of my business secrets."

Mason said, "That's one of the reasons I wanted to get in touch with you before you'd given them permission to go out and pick up your car"

"Well, you were just a little bit late," Kirby said angrily.

"That's right," Mason said, "through no fault of mine. If you'd insisted on waiting for me when they asked you to go to the district attorney's office, I could have gone with you. You knew I was on my way to your house."

"Step on it!" Kirby said impatiently.

"And in case this is bothering you," Mason said, reaching in his pocket, "I took the precaution of removing the sales slip which was given you by the service station when you bought that one-gallon can of gasoline, Kirby."

Kirby snatched at the receipt, then looked at Mason with stormy, suspicious eyes. "And what are you going to do with that information?" he asked.

"Nothing," Mason said. "With some clients, of course,

83

I'd have to coach them what to do, but since you are a businessman and are accustomed to fast thinking, reaching important decisions and all that, I won't have to say a word."

"As a matter of fact," Kirby blurted after a short silence, "that sales slip doesn't mean what you think it means."

"I see," Mason said.

Kirby settled back against the cushions, his eyes narrowed in thought.

Mason said, "For once tell me the truth, Kirby. Did you have an appointment with Dr. Babb Monday night, either with or without this Logan girl?"

"No."

"Is that the truth?"

"Yes."

"It may be important."

"All right, suppose it is. I've told you the truth. Now shut up and let me think. I've got to correlate certain events in my own mind."

Chapter 8

Mrs. Kirby was standing in front of the house as they drove up.

She ran to her husband as Mason turned the car into the driveway.

"John!" she said, "is everything all right?"

John Kirby gave her the genial smile of a successful salesman who is firmly convinced of his own ability to cope with any situation which may arise. "Everything's under control," he said.

She flashed Mason a grateful glance. "You were in time!"

Her husband said, "Mason hurried up there, Joan, but actually there was no need of all the fireworks. I covered the situation with the D.A. and we're buddies. We're just like that."

John Kirby held up his hand with the first and second fingers crossed.

"John," she asked anxiously, "*what* did you tell him?"

"Why, I told him the truth of course. *I* don't have anything to conceal. I picked up a woman and took her to a motel. I registered as husband and wife because that was the only way I could get her a room, but I just registered and then went on. I didn't hang around at all."

"Did they ask you about this woman in some detail?" Mason inquired.

"Why of course, they wanted to know all about her. They have an idea that she's mixed up in an attack on some doctor. They may be able to prove it, too. They found her fingerprints in the motel, and also found some of her finger-prints in this doctor's house."

"You know that this was a murder, John?" she asked. "You knew that this Dr. Babb had died? I heard it on the radio just now."

"They didn't tell me that," her husband said, "but I realized they were investigating something they thought pretty serious, something a little more grave then just an ordinary theft of narcotics. Anyhow I came clean. I told them exactly what had happened. They came and got my car?"

"Yes."

"How did they take it? Did they drive it?"

"No, they towed it," she said. "They were very careful not to touch the interior of the car at all. They wanted to get fingerprints."

"Well, it's all right," Kirby assured her. "I gave them permission. I told them I had another car which we could use. After all, dear, there's no use getting excited about all this."

"Now look," Mason said to Kirby, "you're not kidding anyone except yourself. On Monday night shortly after eleven-thirty, someone committed an assault on Dr. Babb. You'd had some previous dealings with Dr. Babb. A girl was seen running out of Dr. Babb's office. Neighbors can identify her if they see her again. You took that girl to the Beauty Rest Motel and registered with her as husband and wife. The evidence in the case pointed to you but because you're a prominent man the police weren't going to proceed against you until after you had crucified yourself by admitting that you took the girl to that motel.

"Police have checked Dr. Babb's office and found the girl's fingerprints. They checked the Unit Number 5 in the motel and found more of those same fingerprints. By the time they have checked your car and found her finger-prints in your car, they'll be ready to act, regardless of how

86

prominent you may be. They'll have enough evidence against you to hold you as an accessory.

"I've played along with you, hoping that you'd tell me the truth and I wouldn't have to take you to pieces in order to get the true story.

"I don't know how much of this your wife knows, but it's time she knew the whole business. Dr. Babb had a service by which he juggled the birth records so black-market babies could be carried on the birth records as legitimate children. You and your wife subscribed to that service. Ronson was a black-market baby. He still is, despite the fact that the birth certificate registers him as your son.

"The police have been playing with you as a cat plays with a mouse. The reason Hamilton Burger, the district attorney, was so cordial to you is that he felt certain he had you in a trap. He was tickled to death. Not only does he want to solve the case and have the credit of getting a conviction, but he's not at all averse to all the publicity that will go with convicting a wealthy man of murder.

"The young woman whom you took out to Dr. Babb's office was Norma Logan. Actually she's a half-sister of Ronson. She's been interested in him. She knows all about the kind of service Dr. Babb was giving in connection with the black-market babies.

"Now then, I've been given the run-around long enough. Let's have the truth and have it fast, and then I'll tell you what you're up against."

John Kirby looked at Mason with an expression of utter consternation on his face.

"John," his wife said, "did you do that?"

"I drove the girl out to Dr. Babb's place," he said in a low voice, "but you don't need to worry, dear. That girl didn't do anything illegal. She's in the clear and, despite Mr. Mason's gloomy predictions, she's going to stay in the clear. They may be able to prove she went out to Dr.

Babb's office, but that's *all* they can prove, and don't forget it."

Mason stood regarding Kirby with angry eyes, feet spread apart, hands jammed in his trousers pockets.

He said, "You've engaged in the most expensive pasttime known to litigants, that of lying to your lawyer. If you had told me the truth yesterday afternoon, I might have been able to have saved you from a lot of things that are going to happen."

"What's going to happen?" Kirby asked. "I'm in trouble on this thing, Mason, but not in the kind of trouble you think, and not in as deep as you think. Remember this, I'm rather a prominent man in this city. I have influential friends and contacts. I can pull a lot of political wires if I have to."

"Sure you can," Mason said. "That's why they pulled this cat-and-mouse business with you and decided to wait until they had you absolutely hooked before they moved against you.

"It may be they'll be ready to move against you as soon as they find Norma Logan's fingerprints in your car. It may be they'll wait until they've picked up Norma Logan and heard her story."

"They won't hear her story," Kirby said.

"Don't kid yourself," Mason told him. "They'll make her talk."

Kirby shook his head. "If they pick her up, she'll be like a clam, if not for my sake, at least for Ronnie's sake."

"No, she won't," Mason said, "because you've jerked the rug out from under her. You told her to corroborate your story about your picking her up. When she tells that story she's sunk. The police will then have the deadwood on her. They can then convict her of murder. They can convict you of being an accessory."

Kirby ran his hands through his hair. "Damn it!" he said.

"This thing is— How the devil did they learn she was registered at that motel?"

"They learned it the same way they're going to learn a lot of other things," Mason said. "Through good, hard work. Now then, what do you want me to do? Do you want me to represent you, or do you want me to walk out and send you a bill for what I've done to date?"

"Good heavens, no! Don't leave us!" Mrs. Kirby interposed. "Mr. Mason, you *must* represent John and you *must* try to do something to keep all of this about Ronnie from coming out in the papers.

"Ronnie's a sensitive, sweet youngster. He thinks that we are his natural parents, and he has all of the feeling of security which comes from that feeling. If he ever finds out that he's adopted— Well, you either tell a child that he's adopted when he's old enough to start talking things over or you never tell him. To let him have the feeling that he's with his natural parents and then give him that emotional shock is simply terrible."

Mason said, "You could have thought of that, you know, six years ago when you tried to outwit the law."

"Well, quite a few people are in the same boat," John Kirby said. "I found out about Dr. Babb from a friend who's— Well, he's the president of a bank. I can tell you one thing—if any of this hits the newspapers, there will be so much influence brought to bear on the district attorney that he'll wish he'd never started this thing."

"Phooey!" Mason said. "It'll give the district attorney an opportunity for a self-righteous crusade. It'll give him the chance to pose as a fearless public official who hews to the line and lets the chips fall as they will.

"Now then, I want to know one thing, Kirby. Can you keep your mouth shut? When the police come back to arrest you, can you tell them that you've told them your story and you don't intend to discuss it any more?"

"I can if you think that's the thing to do," Kirby said, "but I still think—"

"I know you do," Mason told him, "and I haven't time to argue it with you or discuss it. I'm busy. I'm going to have to do things to protect your son's interest."

Mrs. Kirby said quietly, "Go ahead and protect them, Mr. Mason, and send us the bill. As far as Ronnie is concerned, we'll do anything we can."

"All right," Mason said, turning to her, "now I talked with this Norma Logan. I told her that I wasn't in a position to advise her. I told her to see an attorney. I hope she's done so. I think the attorney will tell her not to talk, not even to give the officers the time of day until we know more about the facts in this case, and about how much they have against her.

"Now then," he said, turning to Kirby, "I'm going to ask you this question once more, and I'm going to tell you now that the whole safety and happiness of your son may depend upon it. Did you make an appointment with Dr. Babb for Monday night?"

"No, I didn't."

"Your name was on his appointment book. How did it get there?"

"I didn't make any appointment."

Mrs. Kirby said hurriedly, "But the name Logan was also on there, Mr. Mason. Couldn't this girl, this Logan girl have made it?"

"That's what I'm trying to get at," Mason said. "Somebody's lying. She tells me she didn't make an appointment. I want to know if you did."

Kirby met his eyes. "Mason," he said, "I've been a fool. I've tried to lie to you when I should have told you the truth. But I'll tell you the truth on this. I did *not* make any appointment with Dr. Babb. I didn't have any contact with Dr. Babb. I talked only with Norma Logan. I was afraid to talk with Dr. Babb because . . . because I thought it might

90

be blackmail. And I'm not too certain even yet that it isn't blackmail."

"Neither am I," Mason said. "That's why I'm feeling my way. When the officers come out to pick you up and tell you you're under arrest for murder, tell them you've made your statement and you're not going to say another word."

"You seem to think they're going to come out and arrest me," Kirby said.

"I know damn well they are," Mason said. "Come on, Della. Let's go."

Mason jerked open the door of his car, said to Mrs. Kirby, "Don't leave the house. I want you to stay here where I can get in touch with you. They may come and place your husband under arrest any time or they may wait awhile. Keep me advised.

"As for you, Kirby, I want to know where you are every minute of the day. I suppose you'll go to your office. It would look better if you did. When you get to your office, telephone me. If for any reason you leave your office, telephone me. I want to be in touch with you at all times."

"When is the critical period?" Kirby asked. 'When will—?"

"As soon as they've processed your car for fingerprints. If they find that girl's fingerprints in your car, they'll be ready to take action. That action will consist in picking you up and shaking you down to find out the girl's identity and her address. If you break down and give them that, they may simply hold you as a witness until they've built up more of a case against the girl. But in the end the result will be the same. They'll charge her with murder and hold you as being an accessory."

"Then you feel I shouldn't tell them anything about the girl?"

"Shorten that sentence," Mason said. "I feel that you shouldn't tell them anything."

Mason slammed the car door, stepped on the throttle, and shot out from the curb.

"Well," Della Street said, "at least now we know what we're up against."

"I'm not so certain we do," Mason said.

"What do you mean?"

"The girl's jacket," Mason said grimly.

"What do you mean? What jacket?"

"Norma Logan's jacket," Mason explained.

"What about it?"

"The mother-of-pearl buttons," Mason said. "You heard Mrs. Kirby describe the girl and the mother-of-pearl buttons on the jacket. How did *she* know about those buttons?"

"Why from her husband, of course," Della Street said.

Mason said, "Then her husband told her something he didn't tell us. He didn't describe the buttons at any time when he was talking to us."

Della Street started to say something, then suddenly caught herself. An expression of complete dismay spread over her features. "Good Lord!" she exclaimed.

"Exactly," Mason commented.

"What are you going to do?"

"We'll wait until the police have arrested John Kirby," Mason said. "Then, when there's no opportunity for him to coach her, we'll have her up in the office and then we may find out what actually did happen."

"Chief," Della Street said, her voice showing her worry, "you're taking too many chances in this thing. That notebook which Norma Logan found and took, the story of the woman who ran out of the house, the mother-of-pearl buttons—Chief, I wish you'd never become involved in this case."

"So do I," Mason said, "but it's too late for that now."

Chapter 9

At eleven-thirty, Mason's phone rang. Della Street picked up the receiver, said, "Yes, who is it, Gertie? . . . I'm quite sure Mr. Mason will want to talk with her. Put her on."

Della Street nodded to Mason. "Mrs. Kirby," she said.

Mason picked up the telephone.

Mrs. Kirby, her voice sounding almost hysterical, said, "It's happened, Mr. Mason. Police came and took John into custody. They said they were picking him up on suspicion of being an accessory to murder."

"All right," Mason told her. "That's that. Do you think he'll follow my instructions and keep quiet?"

"I certainly hope he will. He knows now that the happiness of Ronnie is at stake as well as . . . well I *hope* he'll keep quiet."

"You're not certain?"

"I'm not certain, Mr. Mason. Remember that my husband has been trained to try and explain, to convince, to persuade. If they're clever—"

"They will be," Mason interrupted. "Get in your car and get up to my office just as quick as you can. I'll be waiting. How long will it take you?"

"Twenty or twenty-five minutes."

"Try to make it less than that," Mason said.

Mason hung up the telephone, said, "Well, Della, we're in it now."

Della Street, her eyes showing her worry, lowered her voice. "Chief, that book— Wouldn't it be better to destroy it?"

He shook his head. "Not now. Later on, perhaps."

"Now then, Della, get on the telephone. Cancel any appointments I have for today, and rush Mrs. Kirby in here just as soon as she comes to the office."

Mason pushed back his chair, got to his feet, walked over to the window, jammed his hands down in his trousers pockets and stood looking down at traffic in the street, his concentration such that he was entirely oblivious of everything about him.

Twenty minutes later Della Street opened the door and said, "Mrs. Kirby."

"Bring her in."

"She's here," Della said.

Mrs. Kirby moved past Della on into the office.

"Sit down," Mason said.

She said, "Oh, Mr. Mason, it was terrible! They came out and arrested John. I believe they'd have placed him in handcuffs if—"

"Sit down!"

She eased herself down into the client's chair.

"Now talk," Mason told her.

"What do you mean?"

Mason said, "You knew about Dr. Babb. You participated in the conspiracy at the time Ronnie was supposed to have been born to you."

"I was in on the scheme. I went to Dr. Babb's maternity hospital, so-called, and I did what he told me to about making announcements to my most intimate friends. And, well—there was a period of about six weeks when I kept absolutely out of circulation, when I saw no one. If that's what you call participating I participated."

"When did you first know that there was going to be trouble about this thing?"

"About what?"

"About Ronnie."

"Not until after—well not until after you pointed out the holes in my husband's story."

Mason said, "Your husband came home from a sales meeting. The next morning he told you this cock-and-bull story about having picked up a young woman carrying a gasoline can and you immediately got frightened, rang me up and asked me to cross-examine your husband."

"Why, yes, of course. What's wrong with that?"

"Everything," Mason said.

"I don't think I know what you mean."

"The hell you don't," Mason told her. "You knew there was trouble over Ronnie. You knew it probably before your husband did. You told me about a girl who was in Dr. Babb's office. You said she was wearing a jacket with mother-of-pearl buttons."

"Well, she was."

"How do *you* know?"

"My husband told me."

"No, he didn't. He didn't know anything at all about what kind of buttons were on that jacket. He didn't know much about her clothes. He described them the way a man would describe a woman. You described that jacket the way a woman would describe it.

"Now then, Dr. Babb had an appointment late at night with someone by the name of Kirby. Your husband says he wasn't the one. There are two people in the family by the name of Kirby. Tell me about your appointment with Dr. Babb and try telling me the truth!"

She sat speechless, looking at him in wide-eyed consternation.

"You were out there," Mason said. "How did you happen to be out there?"

"I . . . I was the one who had the appointment."

"That's better," Mason told her. "Now start talking, and for once try to tell me the truth."

She said, "I don't know whether it was my conscience,

or a premonition of impending evil, but I always had the feeling that something was going to happen to Ronnie because of Dr. Babb. My husband would laugh at me and tell me the thing was absolutely foolproof and bulletproof and not to worry, but I always had that feeling. Then Monday I saw a letter addressed to my husband with Dr. Babb's imprint in the upper left-hand corner."

"Where did you see that letter?" Mason asked.

"At the house. My husband gets most of his mail at the office, but some of the personal things, some of the advertisements and circulars and things of that sort come to the house. He usually doesn't pay too much attention to that mail, and sometimes lets it go for a day or so without looking at it."

"All right," Mason said. "I take it you steamed the envelope open."

"I tore the envelope open. It was addressed to my husband and Dr. Babb said that a certain matter which he thought had been concluded a good many years ago had developed ramifications which he thought should be discussed. He suggested that my husband get in touch with him."

"And later on you gave that letter to your husband?"

"I did nothing of the sort. I burnt that letter in the stove."

"You didn't tell your husband anything about it?"

"No."

Mason eyed her thoughtfully. "So then you telephoned Dr. Babb asking for an appointment? Why didn't you tell your husband and let him do that?"

"Because I was afraid he'd try to put too much sugar-coating on a bitter pill. I simply had to know the truth."

"So Dr. Babb gave you an appointment?"

"Yes."

"When?"

"He said to come around eleven-thirty that night."

"That was Monday?"

96

"Yes."

"You didn't tell your husband about that appointment?"

"No."

"Why?"

"Because I didn't want to alarm him. I knew he was going to be at that sales meeting and—well you know how sales meetings are, Mr. Mason. They talk a little business, then put on some so-called entertainment, which you can put in quotes—I guess it entertains the salesmen all right. They get a terrific bang out of it. I felt that I could see Dr. Babb and get home before my husband arrived. Even if I didn't he wouldn't think anything of it because I quite frequently go out when he's tied up with his sales meetings."

"All right," Mason said, "now suppose you tell me exactly what happened out there at Dr. Babb's house."

"I parked my car a block or so from Dr. Babb's office. I walked to his house and went in through the outer door to the reception room."

"That door was unlocked?"

"Yes. But an electric buzzer evidently sounds when you go in because Dr. Babb came to the door leading from the reception room into the inner offices."

"What happened?"

"He said I was early, that I'd have to wait a few minutes. So he let me sit in the waiting room. He said he was in the middle of another matter, that he'd see me as soon as possible.

"So I sat down to wait, and I became terribly nervous. It suddenly dawned on me that the mere fact of my presence in Dr. Babb's office was most incriminating. Suppose he was under investigation by the police, suppose someone who knew me should come in. So I worked myself into a nervous frenzy. I simply couldn't afford to be left there in his waiting room.

"There was a rest room at the end of the office. I explored it and found it had two doors. One of them led into the inner office, and one of them to the outer office.

"I went in that room and kept the door to the outer office unlatched. It was open just a crack so I could see out."

"What happened?"

"Then after a few minutes the outer door opened and this girl came in."

"The girl your husband described?"

"Yes."

"You had a good look at her?"

"Yes."

"Then what happened?"

"Then all of a sudden there was a commotion from the inner office. I could hear blows and the sound of crashing glass."

"What did you do?"

"I opened the door into the inner office. Dr. Babb was lying on the floor. A man who had his back to me was going through the contents of the safe; that is, he was bent over in front of the safe and was throwing books and papers out."

"What did you do?"

"All I could do was scream."

"You screamed?"

"At the top of my lungs. I'm afraid I became completely hysterical."

"And what did the man do?"

"He bolted out to the back of the house."

"You saw his face?"

She shook her head.

"Then what?"

"I realized the man had fled through a back door. My screams had frightened him more than he'd frightened me. So I went to bend over Dr. Babb, and then I thought of this girl in the waiting room. I knew that girl was still in the outer office; at least I thought she was. I didn't want her to see me, so I ran out through the back way, the way the man had gone. I must have been right on his heels."

"Did you see any trace of the man after you got outside?"

"I didn't see anyone. The door from the office led into a sort of operating room. There was a door from the operating room that was open and I ran through that and saw a door which I thought led out to the back yard. It did. I ran through that door.

"I ran out, then steadied myself, took a deep breath, and tried to get myself together. I walked as quietly as possible around the far side of the house, around the yard of the house next door, and then to my car. I drove away from there and went, I guess, about ten or fifteen blocks and then I went all to pieces. I parked the car in at the curb and sat there and cried and shook and cried and finally got hold of myself and drove on home."

"Then what?"

"I undressed and went to bed, and a little while later John came in. I pretended that I was drugged with sleep. I asked him a few questions about the sales meeting and pretended to fall asleep. Actually I was as wide awake as I've ever been in my life, only I forced myself to lie still."

"And your husband?" Mason asked.

"My husband went to bed in his room—"

"You have separate rooms?" Mason asked.

"Yes, separate rooms, with a connecting dressing room and a connecting bath. We leave the door open all the time, but my husband comes in late quite frequently and I'm a light sleeper. He tries not to disturb me."

"Did he go out again?"

"Yes."

"When?"

"It must have been around three o'clock in the morning."

"How long was he gone?"

"About an hour and a half."

"You heard him take the car out of the garage?"

"Yes."

"You didn't ask him anything about that?"

"No."

"What did you do?"

"Well, the next morning I was so nervous I could hardly eat, but I asked my husband about the sales meeting and then he went on and told me this story about the young woman he'd picked up, and I fell for it at first. I thought he was telling the truth. I told him he mustn't leave a young woman like that marooned without any money no matter who she was, that we should drive out there and pick her up, give her some breakfast, and find out what we could do."

"He agreed to that?"

"Very reluctantly. He kept trying to tell me that it wasn't the thing to do, but I insisted it was, so he finally drove me out there. I don't know just when I began to realize that he was lying, Mr. Mason. In the first place, I knew from the way he acted in going out there that he didn't expect to find that woman there at the motel. So then I began to think about how he had gone out around three or four o'clock in the morning, and I felt certain he'd gone back to pick her up.

"However, I didn't say anything. I let him talk, but I kept thinking, and of course I was terribly concerned about Dr. Babb. I kept the radio on while we were driving and a news program came on and I heard about what had happened and heard that the police had taken an appointment book which had the names of Logan and Kirby in it.

"I knew of course, Mr. Mason, that it was my name they were talking about, that I was the Kirby, but I could see from the expression on John's face that *he* thought *he* was the one."

"Go on," Mason said, "what did you do?"

"I turned to John and asked him. I said, 'John, were you

out there at Dr. Babb's last night? Isn't he the same one who helped us with Ronnie?' "

"And what did he say?" Mason asked.

"Then was when I really knew that my husband was lying and knew that we were in bad trouble. He was very glib and very persuasive, the way he is when he's trying to sell someone a bill of goods."

"Then what?" Mason asked.

"Then I didn't know what to do, but I kept thinking things over, and then I telephoned you, and after you said you'd see my husband at two o'clock, I rang him up at the office and told him that I wanted him to go and tell his story to you. I told him that we didn't know but what if this girl was some sort of blackmailer, and if he would tell his story to you it would lay a foundation so that, in case she did subsequently try any blackmail, we could count on your sympathetic cooperation."

"Did you have any trouble persuading him?"

"Some, but not too much. Now that's the story, Mr. Mason. Now I've come clean with you and now you know what we're up against."

Mason's fingertips drummed noiselessly on the blotter of his desk.

She said, "I'm sorry, Mr. Mason, I should have told you all this right at the start. I would have done so if it hadn't been for Ronnie. It's difficult to tell you how I feel about him. I have not only a love for him but a desire to protect him. I'd do anything for him. I'd kill if I had to, to protect him.

"Ronnie is one of the dearest children you have ever seen. He's so poised, has such charm and character—there's something about him even at the age of six that is ... it's hard to describe. It's a very definite quality, a sort of gallantry. When you see him, you'll understand.

"Mr. Mason, we simply must keep him from having the

101

emotional shock that is going to take place if he finds out about his . . . about his adoption."

"Yes," Mason said, "and then when you add to that the shock of having both of his parents mixed up in a murder case, yes, it's one hell of a mess you've dumped in my lap, Mrs. Kirby."

"Well, at least," she said, "I have come clean. I've put all the cards on the table."

"Yes," Mason told her dryly, "now that the police have trumped all your aces, you put your twos and threes in my hand and ask me to carry on the game."

Chapter 10

After Mrs. Kirby left the office, Della Street pulled up a chair and sat down across the desk from Perry Mason.

"Chief, I'm worried."

"Who isn't?" Mason said.

"Where does all of this leave you?"

"In the middle of a legal quicksand. In the first place, I'm not entirely certain whom I'm representing. Ostensibly I'm representing John Kirby. But the thing that he wants me to do above all else is protect Ronnie.

"Now then if we put on the evidence we have, we can get John Kirby out of the mess—at least I hope we can, but in doing that we get Mrs. Kirby right into the middle of a murder charge."

"Are you going to tell Mr. Kirby about his wife being out there?"

"There again," Mason said, "we run up against a problem. It's my duty to tell my client what I know. However, there are some aspects of this case I'm going to have to think over."

"Chief, what worries me is that book."

Mason got up and began pacing the floor, thinking, frowning. Abruptly he stopped pacing, turned to Della Street. "You have that book?"

"I've never told you so in so many words."

"Tell me now. Do you have it?"

"Yes."

"Get it."

"It will take a little time."

"Go get it."

"Now?"

"Now."

Della Street left the office, returned in some five minutes, handed Mason a small cardboard-backed, spiral-bound notebook.

"Now I'm more frightened than ever."

Mason slid the book into the side pocket of his coat. "Forget it, Della, I'll carry the ball from now on."

Della Street said, "You have that book and it's stolen property. Norma Logan isn't your client. The things she's told you aren't confidential communications. You can't justify yourself on the ground of protecting a client—you've taken evidence into your possession, you're concealing that evidence, and the fact that it's stolen property means that you're technically guilty of receiving stolen property. You know what Hamilton Burger, the district attorney, will do if he ever gets an inkling of that."

Mason nodded.

"And," Della Street went on, "it seems to me inevitable that he's going to find out about it."

Mason said, "When an attorney's doing what he thinks is right, Della, he is entitled to take advantage of every technicality in the law. I've told you that I have a certain amount of legal ingenuity, and a certain amount of human ingenuity. I'm going to exercise them both."

"And you're not going to surrender that book to the police?"

"Not in a hundred years," Mason said.

"Then that leaves you in a vulnerable position."

Mason again got up and started pacing the floor. "That appointment book, Della; Dr. Babb wrote the name 'Kirby' in it. It didn't stand for John Kirby but for Joan Kirby.

"He also wrote the name Logan. I've been assuming that meant John Kirby and Norma Logan had a joint appointment. We now know that they didn't.

"Hang it, Della, do you suppose the name Logan didn't mean Norma but meant the boy's father?"

"Good heavens!" Della Street exclaimed.

Mason continued pacing the floor.

"But the father's been dead for six years, Chief."

Mason said, "Get Paul Drake on the phone, Della. Tell him to look up the whole Logan family tree. Let's not jump at any more erroneous conclusions."

Della Street put through the call, relayed Mason's instructions to the detective, then hung up the phone, looked anxiously at Mason.

"Chief, couldn't you go to some good criminal attorney about that book, and—?"

"Why?" Mason asked.

"He could advise you not to turn the book over to the police. Then you'd be acting under legal advice and—"

The phone rang. Della Street scooped up the telephone, listened for a moment, said, "Just a moment, Gertie," then turned to Mason.

"Carver Kinsey is in the office and says he has to see you immediately on a matter of importance."

"Carver Kinsey," Mason said musingly. "To give the devil his full title Carver Moorehead Kinsey, one of the slickest criminal attorneys at the bar. Now what the devil do you suppose *he* wants?"

"I don't know," Della Street said, "but look, Chief, couldn't you at least consult with him, couldn't you ask him to advise you? If you could get some attorney to advise you that it was all right for you to keep that book, then you'd technically be acting under the advice of counsel, and—" She broke off as Mason smiled and shook his head.

"He wouldn't advise me to keep the book, Della."

"Why not?" she asked.

"Because," Mason said, "he knows he couldn't get away with it. He also knows that the bar association is watching him very, very closely. There's one lawyer who is *really* shifty."

"Crooked?" Della Street asked.

"They've never caught him at it," Mason said, "not with anything they could prove, but he's smart and clever and slick. Tell him to come in, Della."

Della went out and escorted Carver Kinsey back to the inner office.

Kinsey was a short, slender individual, who was inordinately proud of his clothes. He kept himself tailored to the minute, and had his hair trimmed every third day. His nails were glistening, his hands were as soft as his eyes were hard.

As someone had expressed it, Kinsey was always trying to improve the appearance of the package, because he knew that the goods inside were rotten.

"Good afternoon, Counselor," Kinsey said.

"How are you, Kinsey?" Mason said, shaking hands. "What brings you up here?"

"Oh, just a little visit," Kinsey said. "I was in the building, so I thought I'd drop in and say hello. After all, we don't see each other too often, but I follow your cases with the greatest interest. In fact, Mason, you might say this is the visit of a disciple to the old maestro. I thought perhaps if I spent a few minutes with you, some of your brilliance and resourcefulness might rub off on me, and I need it. Would it be all right if we dispense with the presence of Miss Street for a few minutes?"

Mason smiled and shook his head. "Miss Street is my right hand. I am too busy to explain all of the ramifications of everything to her, so I let her sit in on all of the conferences and in that way she knows as much about the business as I do. You don't need to worry about her discretion."

"I'm not worrying about her discretion, but I'm worried about that pencil she has a habit of picking up, and that shorthand notebook that gets filled with verbatim transcriptions of conversations."

"Are you going to say something you don't want to have taken down?" Mason asked.

"Yes."

"You aren't going to say anything that you would repudiate afterwards, are you?"

Kinsey met Mason's eyes. "Yes."

Mason smiled. "Well, there's nothing like frankness. Put your pencil away and come over here and sit down where Mr. Kinsey can watch you, Della."

"I'd prefer to have no witnesses," Kinsey said.

"Under those circumstances," Mason told him, "you virtually double my desire to have a witness present."

"Oh, all right," Kinsey surrendered. "I want to talk with you about that Babb case."

"What about it?" Mason asked, his face instantly becoming an expressionless granite-hard mask.

"I'm representing Norma Logan. You told her to go to an attorney. She came to me. Thanks for sending me the business."

"I didn't send her to you," Mason said. "I simply told her to see an attorney. I felt under the circumstances I shouldn't even make any recommendation."

"Well, thanks anyway, Counselor. I got the business."

"Lucrative?" Mason asked.

Kinsey met his eyes. "It's going to be."

"Go on," Mason said.

Kinsey said, "I'm not going to pull any punches with you, Mason, and I'm not going to beat around the bush. I'm an attorney. I'm representing Norma Logan. She doesn't have any money to pay me. I'm in a spot where I've got to cut a corner. I don't do that for chicken feed. I want money."

"And how do you feel you are going to get money?" Mason asked.

"*You're* going to give it to me."

"*I* am?"

"You are. Of course, you'll get if from your client, but I need money."

"How much money?"

Kinsey said, "Let's put the cards on the table, Mason. Your client is a wealthy oil man. He's fighting for his life in a murder case. At the proper time my client Norma Logan can clear him. She can show that he was waiting outside, and that some woman was the one who perpetrated the crime."

"Provided a jury believes her."

"By the time I get done coaching her, even the district attorney will believe her."

"Let's hope so," Mason observed.

"However, that isn't the main thing," Kinsey said. "There's the matter of a notebook which was delivered to Miss Street, Mason."

"Who says so?"

"My client."

"What about the notebook?"

"That notebook is a remarkable record, Mason. An attorney who had that notebook could call on some of the wealthiest families in this city. He could let them know that he had the notebook. He could let them know that they could trust his discretion. Almost overnight he'd find himself in an enviable position. He'd have clients of wealth and respectability. He could quit this rat race of criminal law and move in on oil business, big corporation work. In short, he'd have the world by the tail on a downhill pull.

"That notebook is a legal gold mine, Mason, and there's enough in it for both of us."

"I don't know what you're talking about," Mason said.

"Oh, don't play dumb," Kinsey told him, "and don't be afraid to incriminate yourself. Here, I haven't got any concealed recording devices on me. Take a look."

Kinsey opened his coat, spread his arms wide.

Mason made no move to get up from behind his desk where he was seated. "You and I look at things from a different viewpoint, Kinsey," he said.

"I know, I know," Kinsey said. "You're one of these lucky guys. You defend a client and get him off because he's innocent. I defend a client and get him off because I knock a hole in the prosecution's case somewhere, or get a hung jury. They accuse me of suborning perjury, of bribing jurors and suppressing evidence. You're lucky and smart as hell. *You* can afford to pull all this ethical stuff. *I* can't. I'm in a rat race, and it's going to catch up with me sooner or later. One of these days I'll be disbarred and because of the income tax I can't salt away enough to see me through. This situation that has developed now is the answer to everything. This is a dream come true. You know it and I know it.

"We don't have to pull any blackmail. All we have to do is to let John Doe the big banker and Richard Roe the financier know that we know their son and daughter were respectively the products of Dr. Babb's ingenious scheme for short-cutting adoption proceedings.

"We don't ask for any money. We simply tell these people that we know, that we are, however, very sympathetic and will do what we can to protect their interests.

"They don't pay us any money for blackmail. These people control corporations that are using attorneys all the time. They spend thousands of dollars for lawyers' fees.

"They begin to call on us in connection with their corporation work. We join their clubs. We get in on the ground floor of investments. We become wealthy, respected and influential. The district attorney, who now hates us with an undying hatred, will begin to fawn on us and cultivate our friendship. We'll represent political influence, campaign contributions and political advancement. The Governor will consult us when there's a vacancy on the bench. We'll move into the hallowed inner circles of influence. We'll reek with respectability. We'll get out of this slimy practice of criminal law."

Mason said, "That may be the way you look at it, Kinsey. It's not the way I look at it. The practice of criminal law isn't slimy unless you make it slimy. It isn't a rat race unless you run with the rats. The law gives every person accused of crime an opportunity to be confronted with the witnesses against him, the chance to cross-examine those witnesses, to present his case to a jury. The law clothes him with constitutional rights and safeguards against wrongful conviction, and—"

"Oh, save it!" Kinsey interrupted angrily. "Save it for a jury or a meeting of the bar association. Don't peddle that stuff to me. You've been lucky. You've been shrewd. You've been able to pick innocent clients and get them off by dramatic bits of last-minute legal melodrama.

"But don't kid yourself. Despite the fact that you've represented innocent clients, you've made powerful enemies. The district attorney is after you the same as he's after me. He'd like nothing better than to disbar you and I hold in my hand the means by which he *can* disbar you. Let's be frank, Mason. Let's face the facts."

"What do you mean?" Mason asked.

"You know what I mean. You've received stolen property. All I need to do is to put my client on the stand at the right time. All I need to do is to give a tip to the right people and I can become the fair-haired child while you're finally caught in a legal cul-de-sac."

"You intend to do that?" Mason asked.

"I intend to get money," Kinsey said. "I intend to have a fee. I'm not going to pull the legal chestnuts out of the fire for a rich oil man and have nothing in return except a few pennies from a secretary, or a mortgage on a Ford automobile which isn't paid for.

"I'm playing around with the big money in this thing, and I intend to get some."

"And then?" Mason asked.

"And then," Kinsey said, "I intend to get possession of that notebook. I intend to get the information that is going to make us both rich. I'm not going to hog it. I'm going to share it with you. There's enough there for both of us. Dr. Babb is dead. He left behind that notebook which contained secrets that are worth more than a million dollars, not in blackmail but in legal fees."

"It sounds very much like blackmail to me," Mason said.

"Don't be naïve," Kinsey told him. "There's no one who could touch us with a ten-foot pole on a situation of that sort. We'd be collecting legal fees from clients who annually pay out hundreds of thousands of dollars in legal fees."

"Specifically what do you want now?" Mason asked.

"Now," Kinsey said, "I want a retainer."

"How much of a retainer?"

"Let's not beat around the bush, Mason. I'm not in this business for my health. I want twenty-five thousand dollars *cash*."

"And what do you propose to do in return for that cash?"

"I propose to represent Norma Logan."

"In what way?"

"I propose to handle her case in such a way that she won't be involved in anything, and if your man Kirby comes through with the money like a little gentleman, I intend to handle Norma Logan's case in such a way that it won't embarrass John Kirby and it won't bring out any information about Ronson Kirby that is going to cause any heartache."

"And if you don't get the money?" Mason asked.

"Don't be silly, Mason. You act as though you were trying to get me out on a legal limb. I'm not making any threats. I'm not making any promises. I'm simply telling you that I'm representing Norma Logan, that under the circumstances of this case it will be advisable for John Kirby to give me a retainer of twenty-five thousand dollars now."

"And later?" Mason asked.

"Later," Kinsey said, "you and I will share the information in that notebook."

Mason said, "I'll pass your request on to my client."

"Oh, come off your high horse," Kinsey told him. "Don't pull that dignified stuff. Get on the telephone. Ring up—"

"My client is in custody," Mason said.

"Of course he's in custody. I'm telling you to ring up his wife. She can make out a check for twenty-five thousand dollars without even knowing the money's gone."

"What makes you think so?" Mason asked. "What's your source of information?"

"Kirby himself told my client that he and his wife had a joint checking account of over a hundred thousand dollars, that whenever the balance got below that point his cashier simply diverted enough from the incoming oil royalties to keep the amount at a hundred thousand dollars."

"I'd have to talk with my client," Mason said.

"Well," Kinsey said angrily, "how long is it going to take you to talk with your client?"

"I can't tell."

"All right, what about that notebook?"

"On the notebook," Mason said, "I can give you a definite answer now."

"What is it?"

"If," Mason said, "there exists any such notebook as you have mentioned, and if circumstances developed which placed that notebook in the possession of my secretary or myself, I would exercise every precaution, every bit of ingenuity I could summon to see that neither *you* nor anyone else ever got possession of that notebook or any of the information it contained."

Kinsey jumped to his feet, his face flushed. He hammered the corner of Mason's desk. "Don't think you can adopt that holier-than-thou attitude! Don't think you're so utterly irreproachable! You're in a situation right now where you're violating the ethics of the profession and the law of this state. I can lower the boom on you any time I want to and if you don't snap out of it I'm going to do that very thing."

"You don't need to pound the desk," Mason said. "You don't need to raise your voice and you don't need to waste any more of your valuable time. You've told me your story and there's the door."

"What are you going to do about letting your client pay me a fee?" Kinsey asked.

"I'm going to give *that* matter careful consideration. I'm going to try to do what is for the best interests of my client. Right at the moment, I'm inclined to think that it would be both unwise and unethical for him to contribute a dime to Norma Logan's lawyer. If that should ever come out, it would be a fact which the district attorney could use in attempting to show a conspiracy, a joint purpose in their negotiations with Dr. Babb, whatever those negotiations were. That might tend to crucify my client."

"You damn fool!" Kinsey said. "No one is going to know about it. I told you I wanted the twenty-five thousand dollars in *cash*. I assumed that you were smart enough so you'd see that the payment couldn't ever be traced."

"And once my client did that," Mason said, "you would have a strangle hold over him that—"

"What's the difference?" Kinsey interrupted. "I've got one anyway. I know all about his son."

"You may know," Mason said, "but you've no proof. As far as the records are concerned, Ronson Kirby was born in legal wedlock to John Kirby and his wife Joan Kirby."

"You try to adopt that attitude," Kinsey threatened, "and I'll jerk the rug out from under you. I'll handle this thing in such a way that you'll be the sorriest individual who ever stepped into a courtroom. I'll feather my nest one way or another in this thing, and don't think I won't do it legally.

"I'm charged with protecting the best interests of my client, Norma Logan. If I can protect them through you and through Kirby, I'd say that that was the way to give her the protection she needs. If I can't get you to listen to me, I can damn well get immunity for Norma Logan by having her tell her full story to the district attorney. Her *full* story, mind you, Mason!"

"I heard you the first time," Mason said.

"And your answer?"

"I gave it to you some time ago."

"You have to put my proposition up to Kirby. *You* can't take the responsibility of turning it down," Kinsey said.

"I'll think it over," Mason told him, "and I'm going to put it up to Kirby. Then I'm going to *advise* him that, if he falls for any such scheme as that, he'll have cause to regret it as long as he lives."

Kinsey turned without a word, jerked open the door, and went out.

Della Street looked at Mason's granite-hard features. "Oh, Chief!" she said. "*Why* did this have to happen? I ... I could cry!"

"Crying won't help," Mason said, pushing back his chair and starting to pace the office floor. "Crying won't do a damn bit of good."

"What will do good?" Della Street asked.

"I'm damned if I know," Mason said. "Not at this stage of the game anyway."

"But *what* are you going to do?"

"I'm going right ahead. I'm going to insist that the prosecution go ahead with the preliminary hearing in the case of the People versus Kirby. I'm going to cross-examine witnesses to the best of my ability, and if Carver Kinsey wants to go to the district attorney and purchase immunity for

Norma Logan, I'm going to ... I'm going to—" A grim smile crossed Mason's face. "Frankly, Della, I don't know what I *am* going to do."

Chapter 11

Even a few hours of incarceration had served to melt the aura of self-assurance which had surrounded John Kirby.

The man who sat on the other side of the glass partition and conferred with Mason through a built-in microphone in the heavy plate glass was an entirely different individual from the John Kirby who had breezed into Mason's office to tell him the story of the young woman with the gasoline can whom he had encountered on the road late Monday night.

Mason finished his recital of Carver Kinsey's offer, saying, however, nothing about the notebook.

"He wants twenty-five thousand dollars cash?" Kirby asked.

"That's right."

"And if he gets that he'll see that this Logan girl is a friendly witness?"

"He didn't say that. He gave me to understand such would be the case."

"And if he doesn't get it, she'll go to the district attorney?"

Mason nodded.

"I think we'd better give it to him," Kirby said. "I hate to do it, but . . . I'm fairly well heeled, Mason. I can afford it, and I *can't* afford to take chances."

Mason told him, "I don't think you can afford to do it."

"Why not?"

"I don't think you can afford to get mixed up with that crowd or follow that line of ethics."

"We're not playing with ethics now, Mason. We're facing grim reality. We're facing murder charges. We're facing absolute disaster. We're facing the almost inevitable certainty that our relations with Dr. Babb are going to be publicized."

Mason nodded, said, "This isn't blackmail. It's legal, but it comes pretty close to blackmail. The more I think of it, the more I'm against it. I advise you not to do it."

"I think we should."

"Then get another lawyer." Mason told him.

Kirby flushed. 'Damn you, Mason! You don't leave a man much choice in the matter."

"You have your choice," Mason told him. "Either let me handle the case my way or get some other lawyer."

"Do you always play a no-limit game?" Kirby asked irritably.

"The games I sit in are always no-limit games," Mason told him.

"Well, just what *do* you intend to do?"

"I intend to move for an immediate preliminary hearing. I think we can get it."

"Don't they usually try for delay in cases of this sort?"

"I suppose so," Mason said, "but I think the thing to do is to hit this thing while it's hot. If we have any chance, I want to take that chance before all of this information about Dr. Babb and your son is publicized. If we can't win, let's find out how bad the situation is."

"Suppose it's one where we don't stand *any* chance?"

"You always stand a chance," Mason told him, "provided you're telling me the truth. You never went inside of that house?"

"Absolutely not. What's more they can't prove that I did. All they can prove is that I was connected in some way with a young woman who did go in that house. And I don't think they can actually *prove* that she committed the murder."

117

Mason said, "They don't as yet have the case they want. They have a series of suspicious circumstances and they may be able to marshal enough evidence to get a judge to bind you over for trial. But they don't have the evidence they need to convict you in front of a jury."

"Isn't that all the more reason why we should try to do business with Carver Kinsey?"

"That," Mason said. "is all the more reason why we should *not* do business with Carver Kinsey."

"I've got a lot at stake," Kirby reminded him.

Mason's smile was enigmatical. "*You've* got a lot at stake! You should be in *my* shoes for a while."

"Well," Kirby said resignedly, "I'm not in your shoes, but I am in your hands, Mason. Do what you think best."

"You want me to continue to represent you?"

"Very definitely."

"All right," Mason told him, catching the eye of the guard and signifying that the interview was over, "I'm going to push for an immediate preliminary hearing."

Chapter 12

Sims Ballantine, the trial deputy, who had recently been handling many of the more important preliminary hearings, got to his feet when Judge Conway Cameron called the case of the People versus John Northrup Kirby.

"May the Court please," Ballantine said, "we are ready to proceed with the hearing. I will state very frankly to the Court that I don't know what the evidence in this case will show."

"You mean you haven't discussed the case with the police or the witnesses?" Judge Cameron asked.

"Yes, Your Honor, with *some* of the witnesses."

"Not with others?" Judge Cameron asked.

"We don't as yet know who some of the others are, Your Honor. I'll state very frankly that I would much prefer to have a continuance in this case. If we can have such a continuance it is possible that some matters which are in doubt at the present moment can be clarified. I feel that it may well be advantageous to the defendant to have a continuance."

"And the defense?" Judge Cameron asked, looking at Perry Mason.

"The defendant wishes the prosecution either to proceed with the preliminary hearing or dismiss the case," Mason said.

"Very well," Judge Cameron ruled, "we'll proceed with the preliminary."

He turned to Ballantine. "Do I understand it to be the position of the district attorney's office that it may not have

119

sufficient evidence in its possession at this time to ask for an order binding the defendant over?"

"No, Your Honor, that is not our position," Ballantine said. "We *do* have sufficient evidence on which to ask the Court to bind the defendant over. Whether we have enough evidence at the present time to get a conviction in front of a jury in the superior court is another question. I am stating my position frankly to the Court."

"The Court appreciates frankness," Judge Cameron said. "The Court also would call to the attention of counsel that while there is a rigid rule as to the defendant's rights when a postponement is asked, it is always possible for the district attorney to dismiss the complaint without prejudice and transfer the entire matter to the grand jury where all of the witnesses can be heard before any action is taken."

"I understand, Your Honor, but action has already been taken in this case. A complaint has been filed, and the prosecution feels that to dismiss the complaint at this time might have an adverse effect."

"Very well," Judge Cameron ruled, "but don't think you're going to take this Court on any fishing expedition. If you're not certain of your case, dismiss it, back up and go before the grand jury. That's my suggestion."

"We're certain we can present a strong enough case to bind the defendant over," Ballantine said.

"Then go ahead and put it on," Judge Cameron said sharply. "You understand the rule of law and the Court understands it."

"Joseph Hesper," Ballantine said.

Hesper came forward, took the oath, testified that he was a police officer, that he had been on duty in Radio Car Number 157 on the 5th of the month, that at 11:34 a call had been received stating that there apparently was a disturbance at 19647 Sunland Drive, that he and his partner, George Franklin, had hurried to the house, that they were within a few blocks of the place at the time the call was received, that they followed the best police procedure in dealing with calls of that nature. They took care not to alarm the suspect, they shut off the car motor, as well as shutting off the car headlights when the were a block away. They coasted up to the house, using the hand brake so that they would not give a telltale flash with the red warning brake. As the car was braked to a stop with the hand brake, the witness Hesper had said, "I'll take the front, George, you take the back."

Whereupon in accordance with a routine worked out in such cases, Franklin had dashed around to the back door while the witness had gone to the front door, had started to ring the bell button, then had noticed that the front door was slightly ajar. He had pushed it open, called out that he was a police officer, had received no answer and had entered the house; then as he moved through the rooms and entered the inner office he had found broken glass from a heavy beaker on the floor and a man lying partially on his right side with his right arm outstretched, his left arm doubled, the left hand underneath his breast. There were fragments of broken glass lying about, and the witness had bent over and felt for a pulse. He found that there was a faint, thready pulse, and at that moment he heard his partner, George Franklin, calling out that he had found a man tapping on a window at the back of the house. The witness had thereupon gone to the back door, opened the door, and let in his partner, who was at that time accompanied by one Donald Derby, who, it turned out, was Dr. Babb's handy man. Hesper testified that Derby had a soggy bath towel wrapped around his middle and was shivering as he had just emerged from a shower. The witness had questioned Derby briefly, ordered him to return to his rooms and then had notified headquarters asking for an ambulance and a fingerprint man.

The witness went on to state that a neighbor, a Mrs. Dunkirk who lived next door, had pounded on the front door, seeking admission; that he had gone to the door and had talked with this witness, then had again telephoned headquarters asking for assistance from any radio cars which might be available in nearby territory.

"Cross-examine," Ballantine said.

"You followed your usual routine of police procedure?" Mason asked.

"Yes, sir."

"You checked both the front and the back of the house?"

"Yes sir."

"Then, after calling for the ambulance and asking for a fingerprint man to be sent out, you called again asking for more cars?"

"Yes."

"Why?"

"Because I wanted to pick up a young woman who had been seen running from the house."

"Who saw her?"

"Mrs. Dunkirk."

"Did she describe this young woman?"

"Yes."

"What did she say?"

"Now just a minute," Ballantine interrupted. "We don't want hearsay testimony here. Never mind what she told you."

"I have no objection," Mason said.

"I do," Ballantine said. "Let's not get this record cluttered up with a lot of hearsay. Then pretty quick defense counsel will be wanting to impeach the witness on a lot of immaterial evidence."

"Then you can make an objection," Mason said, "and it will be well taken."

"I'm making it now," Ballantine said.

Judge Cameron smiled. "It's well taken," he said.

"You did, however, talk with this neighbor and from something that you learned from her you did take some action?"

"Yes, sir."

"What?"

"I left my partner George Franklin in charge of the place

while I started cruising around the vicinity looking for this young woman."

"Did you talk with neighbors on both the east and west?"

"I talked with the neighbor on the east first, that is she came over to talk with me, and immediately after that took off looking for this young woman. I didn't talk with the neighbor on the west until sometime later, after I'd given up the search as fruitless. Those people weren't home at the time the assault took place."

"Can you tell us exactly what you did to see that the evidence in the house wasn't contaminated?"

"Certainly. We closed up the house absolutely and we were very careful to touch nothing, to see that no slightest bit of evidence was disturbed. The house is still sealed."

"Was the handy man in the house with you where he could touch things?" Mason asked.

Hesper seemed rather scornful. "The handy man was never permitted in the house. I interrogated him through the back door; then I sent him back to get his clothes on and ordered him to remain in his quarters. It would have been contrary to proper procedure to have permitted *any* person to enter the house before the fingerprint men had tried to find what they could. My partner did the best he could until reinforcements arrived."

"When was that?"

"The ambulance arrived within about fifteen minutes. However, other police cars closed in on the district and joined in the search for the young woman who we felt might still be in the neighborhood."

"How long did that search continue?"

"I would say about ten minutes. By that time we had become satisfied she had eluded us and the other cars went back to their beats. My partner and I turned the Babb case over to the fingerprint men and technicians."

"Then what?"

"Then we started checking the time element. The handy

123

man felt positive Dr. Babb had gone to the back door to call him, had opened the back door, and had then been jerked back by his assailant."

"Now just a minute," Judge Cameron interrupted. "We're getting into a lot of hearsay evidence here. Probably some of it is pertinent, because the question was a very broad general question which called for a statement as to how the witness had gone about checking the time element. Nevertheless this is plainly hearsay."

"But Your Honor," Ballantine protested, "the cross-examiner himself has called for this hearsay evidence. The question very definitely opens the door."

"We're not objecting, Your Honor," Mason said. "We want to know exactly what was done. After all, this is merely a preliminary examination and we feel that Your Honor can disregard evidence which is improper."

"Well, it's a whole lot better not to introduce it in the first place," Judge Cameron said. "However, in the interests of expediting matters, I'll let the witness proceed. Go ahead with the testimony."

"Well," Hesper said, "I'll put it this way. Assuming that last scream heard by Mrs. Dunkirk took place just before the police were notified, and assuming this handy man stood at the window for four seconds—and we were able to estimate that time both by having him re-enact what he had done and by checking the size of the little pool of water which had dripped from him while he was standing in front of the window—we estimated the time interval which had elapsed between screams and the time Derby saw the back door close, as well as the time which elapsed from the closing of the back door until we arrived at the house.

"We followed the wet footprints on the linoleum in Derby's house from the shower to the front window, from the window to where he had gone to grab the towel, and down the stairs. We could, in other words, follow the handy man's route, step for step.

"By making a comparative test with our shoes on, we found that the elapsed time would be between ten and twelve seconds from the time Derby left the bath until he arrived at the back door of the house. However, he was barefoot and when we took our shoes and socks off and made another test we found that we were slowed down materially. This was particularly true at the place where we started down the outside steps from the garage. We were also slowed down materially in crossing the yard. We estimated the barefoot time, if I may so describe it, as being between fifteen and eighteen seconds, and he probably was in the yard about fifteen seconds before we arrived."

"You considered that time element important?" Mason asked.

"Everything is important in connection with good investigative work," the witness said.

"Did you consider the possibility that there might have been some other person in the house who went *out* the back door?" Mason asked.

"We tried to consider *every* possibility."

"Was there something that led you to believe someone other than this young woman you have described had been in the house?"

The witness, suddenly cautious, said, "Well, I'll put it this way. There could have been."

"Could have been what?"

"There could have been some other person in the house."

"Were there any *facts* which indicated some other person had been in the house?"

The witness glanced at the deputy district attorney, shifted his position in the witness chair and said, "No, I won't say there were any *facts*."

"Were any fingerprints found on the back doorknob, on the inside of the door, indicating some person had made a hurried exit?" Mason asked.

"If he knows," Ballantine said.

"Yes," Judge Cameron said, "if you know."

"I don't know. I wasn't present when the knob was tested for prints," the witness said, obviously relieved.

Mason studied the witness for a few seconds, said, "Now I believe you testified that your partner was out at the back, calling for you to open up?"

"Yes."

"And did you open up the back door?"

Again the witness shifted his position.

"Yes, sir."

"And in so doing, superimposed your own fingerprints upon any other which might have been on the doorknob?"

"That calls for a conclusion of the witness, Your Honor," Ballantine objected. "The question is argumentative, it calls for a conclusion of the witness."

Mason said, "This witness has been testifying, Your Honor, as to the best police procedure. He's obviously an expert in that field. I think it's proper cross-examination."

"I'll permit him to answer this question," Judge Cameron said. "It probably calls for a conclusion, but—well, after all, the situation is obvious."

The embarrassment of the witness became apparent. "Well, yes," he admitted. "I probably *should* have told George Franklin to bring his man around to the front door. However, there was a certain element of urgency in his request that I open the back door, and I did it without thinking."

"And thereby left *your* fingerprints on that knob when you did it?"

"Naturally."

"And thereby obliterated the prints of any other person who might have emerged from that door previously?"

"Objected to as argumentative," Ballantine said.

"The objection is sustained," Judge Cameron ruled. "I think we have explored the possibilities of the situation so that it is quite apparent what happened."

"That's all," Mason said.

Ballantine's next witness was Harvey Nelson, who qualified as a fingerprint expert and testified that he had processed Dr. Babb's house for fingerprints, that he had uncovered several latents of a type which he described as promising, that some of those fingerprints—many of them, in fact—were the prints of Dr. Babb, that some of them were the prints of the handy man. But there were, in addition to those, several latent prints which had been developed sufficiently to be identifiable, but as yet they had not been traced to the fingers which had made them.

Ballantine introduced certain particular fingerprints in evidence, and then asked the witness if he had found any other place where those same fingerprints had been made.

Nelson stated that he had found two separate localities where the prints had been made.

"Where?" Ballantine asked.

"One in the automobile belonging to the defendant, the other in Unit 5 of the Beauty Rest Motel."

Ballantine unrolled a map. "I have here a map diagram of the premises. We can have it properly identified, or if counsel wishes, it can be stipulated into evidence."

"I'll stipulate it may go in subject to the right to challenge it if it should subsequently turn out to be incorrect in any detail," Mason said.

"Very well," Ballantine said. "Now will you show the location of Dr. Babb's house and the location of the Beauty Rest Motel on this map?"

The witness did so.

"Assuming that the map is drawn to accurate scale," Ballantine said, "what is the approximate distance in an air line between the two?"

"About seven hundred feet in an air line. Of course, in going by road it is necessary to make some right angle turns, and the distance is somewhat greater."

"How far by road?"

"About twelve hundred feet."

"While you were in Dr. Babb's house developing latent fingerprints, did you observe any particular objects there?"

"Several."

"Did you observe an appointment book?"

"I did."

"Where was that appointment book?"

"On a desk in the corner of the office which I have referred to in my notes as a consultation office. It is not the little room where Dr. Babb was found, but it is a room where there is a desk, some chairs and several bookcases filled with medical books. Therefore, in my notes I referred to it as the consultation office."

"Did you mark this book in some way so that you could identify it?"

"I did."

"I show you a book and ask you if that book contains a mark of identification made by you?"

"It does."

"Will you tell the Court what that book is?"

"That book is the so-called appointment book which I found in the room I have referred to as the consultation office."

"I ask that the book be received in evidence," Ballantine said, "and we'll call the Court's attention to the appointments for the fifth day of this month."

"No objection," Mason said. "I suggest that the appointments be read into evidence."

"Very well."

"There are several appointments during the day," Ballantine said, "but in the evening there are two appointments listed: Logan and Kirby."

"Only those two?" Judge Cameron asked.

"Yes, Your Honor."

"Are there initials or addresses or any other means of identification than the name itself?"

"No, Your Honor, simply the names. If the Court will

notice the appointment book, the Court will see that all of the appointments are made in that way. Simply the last name. No initials, no address."

"Very well," Judge Cameron said. "It may be received in evidence."

"Now then, Mr. Nelson, did you subsequently call on Dr. Babb at the hospital prior to his death?"

"I did. Yes, sir."

"On how many occasions?"

"Three occasions."

"What did you do on the first occasion?"

"I took his fingerprints so that I could have some means of comparing the latent fingerprints by eliminating those that had been made by Dr. Babb."

"And on the second occasion?"

"I heard that Dr. Babb was regaining consciousness. I tried to ask him some questions."

"Did he answer?"

"He did not."

"The third occasion?"

"The third occasion was shortly prior to his death."

"What was his condition at that time?"

"Objected to," Mason said, "on the ground that no proper foundation has been laid. This witness is an expert on fingerprints but not on medicine."

"Well, I will ask you this question," Ballantine said. "What was his apparent condition with reference to being conscious?"

"He was conscious, he could answer questions, but for some reason it was impossible for him to carry on a conversation. He could answer questions yes and no, and he gave us one name."

"What name was that?"

"The name of John Kirby."

"And how did you happen to give you that name?"

"I asked him if he knew who had struck him, and he

said, 'Yes.' I asked him to give me the name and he finally gave me the name of 'John Kirby.' "

"You may inquire," Ballantine said to Perry Mason.

Mason said to the witness, "You stated that he finally gave you the name."

"Yes, sir."

"What names did he give you prior to that time?"

"He didn't give any."

"What happened?"

"We seemed to have some difficulty getting through to him. I would ask him a question several times, and he'd lie there looking blank; then finally the question would reach him and he'd answer yes or no."

"You couldn't tell whether he understood the question?"

"Only by his answers."

"And his answers being only yes or no," Mason said, "there was, I take it, the chance that he only knew you were asking him questions and in trying to answer he used only the two words he was able to use, so there was perhaps a fifty-fifty chance he may have used them incorrectly."

"I don't think so," the witness said.

"I'm asking you about the facts," Mason said.

"Oh, if the Court please," Ballantine said, "this whole examination is argumentative. The question is argumentative. He hasn't qualified this man as a medical expert, nor has he permitted him to qualify himself so that questions of this sort could be answered."

"Nevertheless," Judge Cameron said, "the witness was permitted to testify as to the man's general condition as it was apparent to a layman. I think the question is in order.

"The witness may answer giving his opinion not as an expert but as a layman."

"I think that when he answered the question he was giving the information called for in the question," the witness said. "I reached that conclusion from the nature of his answers. I think we had some trouble reaching him with the questions, but when we did, I think he could answer them and I think he did answer them."

"Now you say that he *finally* gave you the name of John Kirby?" Mason said.

"Yes, sir."

"And that prior to that time he had not given you any name?"

"Yes, sir, that is correct."

"In other words, you asked him several times who did it?"

"We asked him several times if he knew who did it."

"And what happened then?"

"Several times the question went unanswered. Finally in response to the question after it had been repeated some seven or eight times he said, 'Yes.' "

"And then you asked him who did it?"

"Yes."

"And he answered?"

"Yes."

"That question?"

"Yes."

"The first question?"

"No, it wasn't the first question. It was a repetition of the first question."

"How many times was it repeated?"

"Oh, perhaps seven or eight."

"It may have been more than eight?"

"It could have been."

"It might have been as many as twelve?"

"I didn't count the number of times we repeated the question. I was trying to get through to him."

"You asked him over and over who did it?"

"Yes."

"And then waited after each question for an answer?"

"Yes."

"And there was silence?"

"That's right."

"And then finally about the tenth time, or perhaps the thirteenth or fourteenth time, when you asked the question, you got an answer?"

"I don't think it could have been the fourteenth time. I don't think we repeated the question fourteen times. My best recollection is that we might have repeated it about seven or eight times."

"And he finally made a statement which you thought was an answer?"

"He stated the name John Kirby very plainly, very distinctly."

"Wasn't there a certain slurring of speech?"

"Well . . . not to the extent that it wasn't possible to recognize the name. I will say that when his answers were given, they were clear. There was a certain amount of slurring but not any real mumbling."

"Did you at that time know the defendant in the case?"

"No, sir. We didn't get on his trail until after we had made an exhaustive check of car registrations getting the various combinations of letters and figures. We had several cars to check, but as soon as we had this name we found a car that fit the description registered in the name of Kirby, so we got busy almost immediately checking the defendant."

"And they you processed his car for fingerprints?"

"Right."

"And found latent fingerprints of this same person who had been in the unit of the motel and in the house of Dr. Babb?"

"Yes, sir."

"That's all," Mason announced.

"I will call Milton Rexford as my next witness," Ballantine said.

Rexford, a tall, somewhat stooped individual in his early forties, slouched his way to the witness stand, held up his right hand, took the oath, and stood for a moment looking around the courtroom through pale gray eyes. Then he settled himself in the witness chair, gave his full name as Milton Hazen Rexford, and stated that his residence was on Malacca Avenue.

Ballantine introduced a map showing the territory in question and the witness marked a cross on the map to show the place where he lived.

Malacca Avenue was depicted on the map as the street turning off from Sunland on the opposite side from Rubart Terrace, and a half block down the street.

"I wish to direct your attention to the evening of the fifth of this month," Ballantine said to the witness. "That would be Monday evening. Do you remember that evening?"

"Yes."

"Directing your attention to a time shortly before eleven-thirty, what were you doing?"

"I was getting ready for bed."

"You were in the bedroom of your house?"

"Yes."

"Does that bedroom front on Malacca Avenue?"

"Yes."

"Were the lights on in your bedroom?"

"No, sir."

"Why not?"

"Because my wife was already in bed. She'd pulled back the drapes and opened the window so she'd get fresh air. I didn't want to turn on the room lights and shine 'em in her eyes, so I was undressing there by the open window with the lights out."

"Did you see an automobile at that time?"

"I did."

"Where?"

"Well, a good-looking automobile came to a stop right in front of my house. I couldn't figure who was coming to see me at that hour of the night, and—"

133

"Never mind your mental reactions or your conclusions. Just tell us what you saw," Ballantine said.

"Well, I took a good look at the license number before the man turned the lights off."

"Did you see the license number?"

"Yes."

"Do you remember it?"

"I certainly do."

"What was it?"

"JYJ 112."

"Did you see the man who was driving the car?"

"That's right."

"Who was that man?"

"There he sits!" the witness said, raising a long thin arm and pointing with a bony forefinger directly at John Kirby.

"You are now indicating John Northrup Kirby, the defendant in this action?"

"That's right!"

"What did he do after he parked the car?"

"He switched off the lights, and then he just sat there for a second or two, and then some young woman opened the car door and got out."

"Can you describe this woman?"

"I didn't see her so plain. I didn't see her face. She was a woman, that's all I know."

"Can you tell how she was dressed?"

"Sort of light clothes. I mean kind of light-colored, sort of tannish maybe."

"What did she do?"

"She walked up the street toward Dr. Babb's place."

"Then what did you see?"

"Well, I guess it was about maybe, oh . . . six, seven or eight minutes, and all of a sudden here this young woman came down the hill, lickety-split. She jumped in the car and said something to the man, and the lights on the car came on, and believe me, that car went away from there fast!"

"How did it go?"

"Made a U-turn, right slap-bang around, and went off down Malacca Avenue."

"You are certain of your identification that it was the defendant who was driving the car?"

"Absolutely certain."

"When did you next see the defendant?"

"Wednesday."

"Where?"

"At the jail."

"Did you see him by himself, or were other persons present?"

"There was what you call a line-up," Rexford said. "A bunch of people, maybe five or six, all standing up."

"And you identified the defendant at that time?"

"That's right."

"Picked him out of the line?"

"Uh-huh."

"Cross-examine!" Ballantine snapped at Perry Mason.

"You sat there by the bedroom window looking out at the car?" Mason asked.

"That's right."

"And you saw a woman run back to the car?"

"That's right."

"You said she was running fast?"

"That's right."

"I believe you said, 'lickety-split'?"

"Uh-huh."

"That means fast, does it?"

"I always figured it did."

"And what did she do?"

"She whipped the door open, jumped in the car, said something to the man, and away they went!"

"The bedroom window was open?"

"That's right."

"Could you hear what she said to the man?"

"Not at that distance."

"Was the car door open or closed when she said something to him?"

"It was closed."

"You couldn't hear the words?"

"No."

"Could you hear voices through the closed car door?"

"No."

"Then how did you know she said something to him?"

"Well, what made him go chasing away like that if she didn't say something to him?"

"Did you see her turn her head toward the man and speak to him?"

"No, the car was dark. But a moment later, the lights on the car came on and I could see the two of them in there when the car went around in a U-turn. Believe me, he sure whipped that car around!"

"The only time you saw the man in front of your house he was seated behind the steering wheel of an automobile, wasn't he?"

"That's right."

"When you identified him in the line-up, you didn't identify him sitting down. You identified him standing up."

"Uh-huh."

"You could see the rear license number when the car came to a stop?"

"Yes, sir."

"Then the car wasn't directly in front of your bedroom window when it came to a stop, but must have been some distance up the street. Otherwise you wouldn't have been able to have seen the rear license plate?"

"That's right."

"So the person who was in the driver's seat wasn't where you could see his profile. You were looking at the back of his head, weren't you?"

"Well, kind of quartering, I guess."

"The man who was behind the steering wheel was on the side away from the curb?"

"Right."

"The right side of the car was the side nearest your house. The left side was the side toward the street?"

"Uh-huh."

"Was the man wearing a hat?"

"I believe he was."

"Aren't you certain?"

"Well, it's kind of hard to tell. It wasn't easy to see."

"When the lights were turned off in that car, it was rather dark in the interior of the automobile?"

"Right."

"There's a street light up on Sunland Drive?"

"There's a street light, but it didn't shine inside the car so much. It was hard to tell whether the driver had a hat on or not."

"Couldn't you tell when the lights of the car were on?"

"I suppose I could. I just can't remember whether he had a hat on or whether he didn't."

"You did look at the license plate on the automobile?"

"Absolutely."

"And you're sure of the license number?"

"Positive."

"How long was it after the car came to a stop before the lights were turned off?"

"Oh, no time at all. Just maybe a second or so."

"And during that time you were wondering who was stopping in front of your place?"

"That's right."

"You thought perhaps it was someone who might be coming to see you?"

"Right."

"So you paid particular attention to the license number?"

"I already said I did."

"You were looking at that while the lights were on?"

137

"Yes."

"Do you want us to understand that you were looking at the license plate all the time the lights were on?"

"Right."

"So you weren't looking at the man who was driving the car?"

"Well, I looked at him afterwards."

"That was *after* the car lights had been turned off?"

"Right."

"So you later identified the defendant while he was standing up in a line-up, yet the only time you had previously seen him he had been seated in an automobile where you only had a quartering view of his head under such lighting conditions that you couldn't tell whether he had a hat on. Is that right?"

"Objection, argumentative," Ballantine said.

"Overruled!"

The witness fidgeted in the chair.

"Is that right?" Mason asked.

"I guess so."

"No further questions," Mason said.

"That's all," Ballantine said. 'No further questions."

"Donald Rufus Derby," Ballantine said.

The handy man came forward and was sworn. He testified that he had been taking a shower, that he had heard a woman scream, that he had shut off the water in the shower bath, dashed to the window overlooking Dr. Babb's house, had seen the back door closing, had hurried to the towel rack, thrown a towel around his middle, and dashed down the stairs.

By the time he had crossed the cement apron in front of the garage and reached the back door of the house, the door was closed and the spring lock in place. He had pounded on the door with his knuckles, and had received no answer and had heard no sound from the inside of the house. He had then gone around to the side window and was tapping on that side window when an officer had grabbed him from behind.

He had thereupon explained the situation to the officer who had held him for a few moments while the other officer opened the back door. The witness had then been sent back to his apartment to get some clothes on and wait until the officers had finished with their inspection of the premises. They had then examined him in some detail, and had conducted tests to determine the time element.

"Cross-examine," Ballantine said to Perry Mason.

"You reached the window just in time to see the back door of Dr. Babb's house closing?" Mason asked.

"Yes, sir."

"Did you see anyone running out of the back door?"

"No, sir."

"Did you see anyone at all down there in the yard?"

"No, sir."

"If someone had run out of the back door just before you got to the window, could you have seen that person?"

'I've been thinking it over," the witness said. "I don't think anybody could have got out that door and got around the house and out of my sight before the door closed. My own idea is that Doc Babb was trying to call me and—"

"Never mind your ideas," Ballantine interrupted sharply. "Simply listen to the questions and answer them."

"No further questions," Mason said.

Judge Cameron said. "Just a moment, gentlemen. I'm sorry that we were late in starting this hearing. However, there was another matter on the calendar which had to be disposed of. I notice that it is now the hour for the afternoon adjournment. Court will take a recess until tomorrow morning at ten o'clock. The defendant is remanded to custody."

Chapter 13

Della Street was waiting for Perry Mason in the office.

"How did the case go?" she asked anxiously.

"So-so," Mason said. "They have a witness who saw Kirby drive up, park his car, and let Norma Logan out. He saw Norma Logan take off in the direction of Dr. Babb's house, and then after a few minutes come running back lickety-split, jump in the car, say something to Kirby and Kirby took off in a hurry."

"Oh-oh," Della said in dismay.

"That means," Mason explained, "that they have a pretty good prima-facie case *provided* they can show that Norma Logan hit Dr. Babb on the head. And that they *can't* show.

"The handy man *thinks* Dr. Babb got as far as the back door and opened it to call to him, but we know that Dunkirk saw the back door closing just after some unidentified man, closely followed by Joan Kirby, had dashed out.

"Now then, under those circumstances, I can call Motley Dunkirk to the witness stand, prove that he saw some woman running out of that back door, and knock their case against Norma Logan into a cocked hat.

"That starts the police on a brand new investigative tangent, but gets Joan Kirby involved in the killing."

"Do you think they can find out this woman was Joan Kirby?" Della Street asked.

"I'm wondering if I dare take a gamble on that. However, I think they'll find out all right. Did we hear anything from Carver Kinsey, Della?"

"Not a peep."

140

"Well," Mason said, "he's sitting tight. He hasn't gone to the district attorney as yet."

"How do you know?"

"How do I know?" Mason asked grinning. "I know because Sims Ballantine, the trial deputy, was conducting the hearing. The minute Carver Kinsey breathes a word to the police or the district attorney you'll see Hamilton Burger come striding into the courtroom and when he does that will mean the fat is in the fire."

"But Norma Logan doesn't know that it was Mrs. Kirby who was in the house," Della Street said.

"Not by name," Mason said. "But she can give a pretty good description.

"So far the case hasn't attracted too much newspaper attention. A prominent businessman is accused of murder, but the developments have been taking place with such rapidity that the public hasn't had its interest whipped up to a point where sob sisters will start interviewing the wife, where newspaper artists will start making sketches, and all of that.

"When that happens Norma Logan is going to see photographs of the wife, she'll see artists' sketches, and above all she'll talk to Carver Kinsey. Kinsey will note the name 'Kirby' in the appointment book, will suddenly put two and two together, and then he'll *really* be in a position to make demands."

"Then what will happen?"

"I'm darned if I know," Mason admitted. "What about Paul Drake? Did he get anything on the Logan family?"

"He sure did. I have it all right here. He looked up Norma Logan's birth certificate, found out the name of her father, and has had men working getting all the information he could.

"There's no question about the father having gone up into the upper Amazon, and he was never heard of after that.

"But here's something, Chief, that's significant: the uncle, that is, the father's brother, is Steve Logan."

"Who's Steve Logan?" Mason asked.

"The big used-car dealer," she said. "Remember all the television advertisements with the slogan, 'Stick by Steve,' 'Buy a used car from Steve Logan, run it for a year, trade it in on another used car, and have the cheapest mileage transportation in the country.' "

"Oh yes, I place him now," Mason said. "Steve Logan, the one who sticks by his customers; you stick by Steve and Steve sticks by you. So he's Norma Logan's uncle?"

"That's right, and Dr. Babb was one of Steve's customers. Dr. Babb had gone into semiretirement. He was trying to keep costs down wherever he could, and he had been buying cars from Steve Logan for three years. He'd pick up a pretty good used car, drive it for a year, go back to Steve and turn it in. I guess there's something to that slogan all right, because apparently Steve made him pretty good deals."

"How did Paul find out all this?" Mason asked.

"I don't know. He had a lot of men out, but I know he traced the registration on Dr. Babb's automobile to find out about Dr. Babb and knew he purchased it through Steve Logan."

"I see," Mason said frowning. "That may complicate the situation, Della. There's a good chance that the Logan appointment on Dr. Babb's books for Monday night was an appointment with Steve Logan. How does Norma get along with her uncle? Does anybody know?"

"That nice shiny car she had was purchased through him," Della Street said.

Mason said, "I think we want to talk with Paul. I—"

He broke off as Paul Drake's code knock sounded on the door.

Mason opened the door and Drake came in.

"Hi, Perry, how's the case going?"

"Sixes and sevens," Mason said. "Della was telling me about your report on Steve Logan, Paul."

"Well, I've got something else," Drake said, "and this may help you."

"What?"

"Logan was out at Dr. Babb's place Monday afternoon."

"Steve Logan?" Mason asked sharply.

"That's right."

"Doing what? Do you know?"

"Sure I know," Drake said, "there's no great secret about it. He was getting specifications on the little garden out there in back, particularly on the goldfish pool."

"Why?"

"Because he likes it. He wants to put in something similar in his show windows. It's his idea that people will walk right by an inanimate display but will always stop to look at something that's moving. He feels that a goldfish display will attract people if the display is made sufficiently attractive."

"How did you find this out?" Mason asked.

"Just fooling around and asking questions in the neighborhood. The neighbors on the west told me about this one. No one's bothered to talk with them very much because they were out at the time the assault took place. They came back from a movie and arrived just about the time the ambulance did. The name is Olney. Mr. and Mrs. Grover Olney.

"However, these people are acquainted with Steve Logan by sight, and they saw him out there taking measurements in the back yard, getting a plan of the goldfish pool and the way the water runs into it.

"You see, water has to be aerated to keep goldfish happy and healthy and this handy man out there has built up quite an ingenious little pathway for the water to follow with little miniature waterfalls, and all of that, and then it flows into this big goldfish pool, is drained out, pumped back into the channel and down through the waterfalls again. The whole thing is handled with a little electric motor."

"Does it run all the time?" Mason asked.

"No," Drake said, "Dr. Babb used to shut it off when he went to bed, then turn it on in the morning. The sound of running water interfered with his sleep. He didn't like it."

Mason said, "That's interesting. I guess no one has ever thought to find out whether the motor had been shut off or not on Monday night."

"Apparently it was shut off," Drake said. "Incidentally, Perry, there's one other person who is interested in goldfish and that's Gertrude, the niece who's visiting the Dunkirks up on the hill.

"Mrs. Dunkirk you know was the one who saw the woman running out of the house."

"Okay," Mason said, "what have you found out about Gertrude, Paul?"

"Gertrude is a problem. I can find out more about her if you want. She's been in some sort of scrape and she's planning to stay with the Dunkirks for three months. While she's staying there, she's keeping out of circulation.

"There's something funny about that whole business. She is nervous, restless, and while she doesn't go out any and mingle with the other young people, she's sixteen, unmarried and—well, it's a hell of a thing to say, Perry, but these neighbors on the west gave her a good once-over and *they* think she's going to have a baby."

Mason and Della Street exchanged glances.

"And she hangs around Dr. Babb's back yard and the goldfish pool?" Mason asked.

"Yes, she got acquainted with Dr. Babb and—I suppose you knew the Dunkirks knew Babb before they moved into the neighborhood."

"I know," Mason said. "Where was Gertrude during the commotion out there Monday night, Paul?"

"Playing the piano like mad," Drake said. "Neighbors

farther up the hill who didn't even hear the screams heard the piano banging away."

Mason became thoughtful. "I wonder," he said, "if—"

Knuckles pounded on the corridor door to Mason's private office.

Mason frowned. "See who it is, Della. Tell whoever it is that I'm engaged in the trial of a case, that the office is closed and I can't see anyone."

Della Street opened the door a crack, said, "Mr. Mason is engaged in the trial of a case and . . . oh, hello, Mr. Kinsey."

Carver Kinsey pushed the door open with the easy assurance of one who is completely immune to rebuffs.

"Hello, Drake," he said. "How's the old sleuth coming? Hi, Mason! How's the case?"

"So-so," Mason said.

Kinsey made himself at home, drew up a chair, took out a cigarette, lit it, blew out the match with a smoky exhalation, grinned at Mason and said, "Let's talk some more."

Drake quickly sized up the situation, said, "Well, Perry, I'll keep busy on this angle and see if I can find out anything else."

"Stay with it," Mason told him.

Drake left the office.

Kinsey said, "Well, Mason, I'm at the place where I have to have a showdown."

"As far as I'm concerned, you've already had it," Mason said.

Kinsey said, "You're playing a deep game, Mason. I don't know what it is but I want you to know that I don't intend to let you off the hook.

"Norma tells me there's no question that Babb was murdered by some woman who must have been in the inner office when she arrived, some woman who ran out of the back door.

"There's an automatic door-closing device on that back

door. The handy man saw the door closing. He doesn't think that anyone could have run out but he has to admit it's a possibility. Of course, he thinks Dr. Babb was going to the back door to call up to him to come down. Naturally he would think that, what with all the screaming and stuff."

Mason stretched and yawned.

"Therefore," Kinsey went on, "you have a lead-pipe cinch. You only need to produce Norma Logan, put her on the stand, have her tell her story, and the case against John Kirby goes out the window."

"Provided they believe her," Mason said.

"I've got her coached," Kinsey said. "They'll believe her. She'll tell her story embellished by cheesecake, tears and corroboration."

"What corroboration?" Mason asked.

Kinsey grinned. "Leave it to me."

"And so?" Mason asked.

"And so," Kinsey said, "we've reached the end of the trail, Mason. I want the information that's in that book. I'll share it with you. You can keep whatever fee you receive for getting the case against Kirby thrown out of court."

"You're *so* good to me," Mason said.

"Damned if I'm not," Kinsey retorted. "Actually the books belongs to my client," Kinsey went on. "I could hold the whole thing as my client's property."

"Where did your client get it?" Mason asked.

Kinsey grinned. "She stole it, if you come right down to it. But you know something, Mason?"

"What?"

"She *could* be in error on that. It *could* happen that she found the book on the sidewalk where someone who had run out of Dr. Babb's house ahead of her could have dropped it. Having found the book that way, it wouldn't be stolen property, and she wouldn't be obligated to return it to anyone unless there was a positive and complete identification, which under the circumstances can't be made."

146

Mason shook his head. "I'm not buying any part of that, Kinsey."

Kinsey's face darkened. "You might consider your own position in this thing, Mason. Right now you're not only concealing evidence, but you have stolen property in your possession. Certain people that I know of would like very much to work things up on that basis."

"Would they indeed?" Mason asked. "If, as you now suggest, your client found the book on the sidewalk I wouldn't be guilty of anything in holding the book."

"My, but you're bright!" Kinsey said. "You get the idea very rapidly. I haven't suggested as yet to my client that she might have found the book on the sidewalk, but I have impressed upon her that she's going to go to prison for a long, long time unless she does *exactly* as I tell her."

Mason said, "I get your idea, Kinsey. I got it the first time. I gave you your answer the first time. Now Della Street and I are going to dinner. Would you mind getting the hell out of the office?"

Kinsey got to his feet. "You know, Mason," he said, "you always did underestimate me."

"Possibly," Mason said.

"You think I'm afraid to make a move," Kinsey said. "You think that I don't dare to approach the district attorney because the district attorney hates me almost as much as he hates you.

"I'm going to tell you something, Mason. I'm a damn sight smarter than you give me credit for being. By the time I get done with this thing, I'm going to be sitting on top of the heap."

"Go ahead and sit on it," Mason said, getting to his feet, "but get the hell out of here before I throw you out."

"Okay, okay," Kinsey said, bowing and smiling at Della Street. "I'll be seeing you one of these days, Mason."

Kinsey opened the door and vanished.

Della Street's anxious eyes appraised Perry Mason. "Chief," she said, "I'm shivering in my shoes."

Mason's eyes were slitted with concentration. "Forget it, Della," he said. "We don't have any other choice in the matter. We can't do business with anyone like that. Hang it! Della, this thing all ties together."

"What?"

"The Durkirks' niece is wild. She got into trouble. The parents were frantic, so the Dunkirks told them about Dr. Babb. Dr. Babb had gone into semiretirement, but for his friends the Dunkirks he was willing to go into business once more.

"So Gertrude came to stay with her aunt and uncle. Circumstances are such that she had to keep pretty much to herself. The whole thing begins to add up."

"I know," Della Street said, "but what's going to happen tomorrow morning? What's going to happen if Hamilton Burger should walk into court and accuse you of having stolen property in your possession and what would happen if Norma Logan has been so thoroughly hypnotized by this shyster lawyer that she goes on the stand and backs up his story?"

"That," Mason said, "is a bridge we'll cross when we come to it. So far Kinsey has been bluffing. He wants that notebook. If he goes to Hamilton Burger—well, he might make a trade with Burger. Burger *might* agree to turn over the book to him in return for getting something he can use against me. But there's one thing none of them have taken into consideration, Della."

"What's that?" she asked.

"The technical rules of evidence," Mason said.

Chapter 14

Perry Mason had paced the floor of his apartment for some two hours before retiring, then, after he had gone to bed, had tossed and turned for another hour before sleep finally came to him.

That sleep was interrupted at about three in the morning by the strident, insistent ringing of the telephone bell. The number of that unlisted telephone was known to only three people in the world: Perry Mason, Della Street, and Paul Drake, the detective.

Mason groped for the light switch, fumbled with the telephone, said sleepily, "Hello."

Della Street's voice, sharp with urgency, said, "Chief, something's happened!"

The note in her voice snapped Mason to instant wakefulness.

"All right, Della, what is it?"

"Officers pounded on my door a few minutes ago."

"Go on," Mason told her.

"I put on a robe, got up and demanded to know who it was. They told me it was the law. Finally I opened the door. They pushed a subpoena into my hands. A *subpoena duces tecum*, calling for a cardboard-backed notebook which was the property of Dr. P. L. Babb. I'm ordered to appear in Judge Cameron's court at ten o'clock and to have the notebook with me. What do I do?"

Mason said, "Turn out your lights, go back to bed, and go to sleep."

"Heavens, Chief! I couldn't sleep now. I'm ... I'm

149

frightened. That means Kinsey has gone to the district attorney."

"All right," Mason said, "let me handle it. Take a glass of hot milk, go to bed, and forget it."

"Is it all right?" she asked anxiously.

"It's all right," Mason assured her. "Sit tight, Della. Get a good sleep. Don't be worried."

Mason had hardly hung up the telephone before the buzzer of his apartment sounded. The buzzer was supplemented by pounding knuckles on the door.

Mason opened the door.

A uniformed officer pushed a paper into his hands. "A *subpoena duces tecum*," he said. "Case of People versus Kirby, Judge Cameron's court, ten o'clock today. G'-by."

"Thank you, officer," Mason said.

"Don't mention it," the officer told him. "Sorry I had to get you up, but those were orders."

"Quite all right," Mason said closing the door.

The lawyer sat on the edge of the bed, tapped a cigarette on his thumbnail, snapped a match into flame, lit the cigarette, inhaled deeply, then regarded the carpet with frowning concentration.

Again the telephone rang.

Mason picked it up. "Hello, Paul," he said.

Paul Drake's voice showed surprise. "How did you know it wasn't Della?"

"She just called."

"I see. Did they serve her?"

"Uh-huh."

Drake said, "My man called me just a few minutes ago. I wanted to warn you so you could keep out of the way and get Della into hiding if you wanted to. That Logan girl has told the D.A. one hell of a story."

"What happened?" Mason asked.

"Well, of course, I'm getting it from an underground pipeline," Drake said. "I don't have any details, but here

150

are the general facts: Carver Kinsey is attorney for Norma Logan. Now get this, Perry, she was the mysterious girl who was seen running out of Dr. Babb's house at the time of the murder.

"Kinsey went to the D.A. about eight o'clock last night. He sold Hamilton Burger a bill of goods. Burger is reported to have made a deal with Kinsey by which Norma Logan will be let off the hook if she gets on the stand and tells her story.

"All hell is going to break in that case at ten o'clock this morning and you're going to be in the center of it.

"Now then, is there anything I can do?"

"I don't think so, Paul."

"I sure hope you know what you're doing," Drake said.

"So do I," Mason told him. "Thanks for calling, Paul." Mason hung up, dressed, started pacing the floor.

Chapter 15

Word had passed like wildfire that fireworks were scheduled to go off in Judge Cameron's court, and the courtroom was pack-jammed with interested spectators and newspaper reporters.

Judge Cameron surveyed the crowd with uncordial appraisal. His manner plainly indicated that he wondered what sudden, unexpected turn of events had caused this surge of interest.

It was also apparent that Hamilton Burger, the district attorney, had now taken personal charge of the case.

As Judge Cameron called the court to order, Hamilton Burger said, "Your Honor, the prosecution desires to call Miss Della Street to the stand. Miss Street is a hostile witness. She is the secretary of Mr. Perry Mason who is representing the defendant."

Judge Cameron said sharply, "You can't do that, Mr. Prosecutor. Any communication made by a client to an attorney is confidential and the same rule holds good for the confidential secretary of an attorney."

"I'm not trying to get testimony concerning a communication, Your Honor. I am trying to recover stolen goods."

"Stolen goods!" Judge Cameron exclaimed.

"Stolen goods!" Hamilton Burger repeated. "We propose to show that certain personal property of Dr. Babb was stolen from his office and that this property was turned over to Miss Street. We have had a *subpoena duces tecum* served upon both Miss Street and Mr. Mason."

Judge Cameron rubbed his hand over the top of his head. "This is most unusual," he said. "It is a most unusual procedure."

"It is a most unusual situation," Hamilton Burger retorted. "I have some authorities if the Court would care to listen to those citations. A privileged communication relates only to disclosures which a client makes to an attorney for the purpose of securing advice as to his legal rights. It does not stretch so far as to give an attorney immunity from responsibility when he participates in concealing evidence, committing a crime, or receiving stolen property.

"In fact, there are exceptions to the rule in regard to confidential communications made to an attorney. There is a long line of authorities on the subject and I am prepared to quote a list of citations supporting what I am trying to do."

Judge Cameron said, "Well, let us proceed in an orderly fashion. You may call Miss Street to the stand, and then ask her certain questions. Specific objections may then be made to those specific questions, and the Court will make specific rulings on each objection. Is Miss Street in court?"

Della Street arose.

"Come forward and be sworn, Miss Street," Judge Cameron said, not unkindly.

Della Street walked forward, held up her hand, was sworn, gave her name and address to the court reporter, and seated herself on the witness stand.

"Miss Street," Hamilton Burger said, "you are employed by Perry Mason?"

"Yes, sir."

"And have been so employed by him for some time?"

"Yes, sir."

"In the capacity of confidential secretary?"

"Yes, sir."

"Are you acquainted with Norma Logan?"

"I have met her."

"Did you see her on Tuesday the sixth of this month during the early part of the evening?"

"Yes, sir."

"Who was with you at that time?"

"Mr. Mason."

"You had a conversation with Miss Logan?"

"Yes, sir."

"To your knowledge is this Miss Logan a client of Perry Mason?"

"Not to my knowledge."

"Did Mr. Mason go to her in search of information rather than in answer to a request from her?"

"Yes."

"Now then," Hamilton Burger went on triumphantly, "in that conversation which took place that night, did Miss Logan tell you that she had stolen a certain notebook from the premises occupied by Dr. Babb on the evening of Monday, the fifth of this month? Answer that question yes or no."

"Just a moment," Mason said. "We object to that question, if the Court please, on the ground that it calls for a privileged communication."

Hamilton Burger arose ponderously. "Now, Your Honor, I am prepared to submit authorities on that point. In the first place, Mr. Perry Mason was there just as any other citizen would be there. He was representing the defendant, John Northrup Kirby. That was the reason he went there. He was trying to get evidence for Kirby. He was *not* representing Norma Logan in any way. He was not acting as *her* attorney. Any communication which was made to him by Norma Logan was not a communication made to her attorney. *She* had not retained him. *She* does not look upon him as her attorney; in fact, he could not be her attorney because of the fact that he is representing the defendant

Kirby in this case, and there would be a conflict of interest as between Kirby and Norma Logan.

"If the Court please, we are now prepared to show exactly what happened on the night of the fifth. We are prepared to prove that the defendant in this case is an accessory before, as well as after, the fact to murder, that he transported Norma Logan to the scene of the crime, that he waited for her return, that he then took her in his automobile and hurried her to a motel where he registered under a fictitious name as husband and wife, that thereafter he concocted a story about finding a woman who was carrying a gasoline can to a car which had become stalled, and which subsequently apparently was stolen.

"He told this story in order to account for the fingerprints of Norma Logan in his car. Subsequently in order to substantiate that purely synthetic story still further, he produced a red gasoline can which he said was the gasoline can the young woman had been carrying.

"If the Court please, we are now prepared to show that the gasoline can was a fabricated piece of evidence *and that the fingerprints of Mr. Perry Mason appear on that gasoline can.*"

Judge Cameron looked at Perry Mason. "Do you desire to be heard, Mr. Mason?"

"On what charge?" Mason asked. "Am I being charged with planting evidence in this case in the form of a gasoline can?"

"You certainly are," Hamilton Burger roared, "and when I take the matter up with the grievance committee of the bar association, you'll be charged formally."

"Because my fingerprints were on the can?" Mason asked.

"You know what I'm talking about," Hamilton Burger said.

"Did you personally examine that gasoline can?" Mason asked.

"I certainly did!" Hamilton Burger retorted. "I know what I'm talking about in this case. I personally saw that gasoline can. I personally examined it. I had it in my personal possession. It is in my personal possession now!"

"Then," Mason said urbanely, "doubtless *your* fingerprints are on it, and, if that is the sole criterion of guilt, I can prefer charges against you before the grievance committee of the bar association."

Hamilton Burger's face purpled.

Judge Cameron flashed a quick smile, then rapped for order. "It would seem that the gasoline can is entirely outside the issues we are here to try at the present time. At least, it is outside the scope of this question.

"Is it your contention, Mr. Mason, that you were representing Norma Logan in any way, or that you are now representing her?"

"No, Your Honor."

"Then it would seem that the question is not subject to objection on the ground that it calls for privileged communication."

Mason said, "The question is further objected to, Your Honor, on the ground that it is argumentative, calls for a conclusion of the witness and calls for hearsay testimony."

Judge Cameron turned to the court reporter. "Will you read the question, please?"

The court reporter read the question: " 'Now then, in that conversation which took place that night, did Miss Logan tell you that she had stolen a certain notebook from the premises occupied by Dr. Babb on the evening of Monday, the fifth of this month?' "

Judge Cameron said, "As the question is phrased, the objection will be sustained."

156

Hamilton Burger took a deep breath. "Did Norma Logan give you a pasteboard-backed notebook that night, Miss Street? You may answer that question yes or no."

"Now just a moment," Mason said. "That question is objected to on the ground that it is incompetent, irrelevant and immaterial if the Court please. Unless the district attorney *first* shows that this notebook has some bearing on the issues in the case at present being tried before the Court, it is completely irrelevant. Miss Street may have received a hundred things last Tuesday night from a hundred different people."

"The objection is sustained," Judge Cameron said.

"Oh, Your Honor!" Hamilton Burger said. "This is grasping at straws. This is taking advantage of every technicality in the book. This is—"

"The Court has ruled, Mr. Prosecutor," Judge Cameron said. "The objection is based upon technical grounds, but nevertheless the objection is well taken."

"Well," Hamilton Burger blurted, "Norma Logan told you at that time she had stolen this notebook from Dr. Babb's office, didn't she?"

"Objected to," Mason said, "on the ground that the question calls for hearsay testimony."

Judge Cameron smiled. "Quite obviously the objection is well taken."

Hamilton Burger said, "If the Court please, I want that notebook produced. I can assure the Court, as a prosecutor in this case, that that notebook is highly pertinent to the issues involved. I can assure the Court that the issues which Mr. Perry Mason is avoiding with all of the legal agility at his command are issues which are pertinent and vital to the determination of this case."

"Well, keep your temper and don't shout at the Court," Judge Cameron snapped. "Go ahead and ask your questions."

"Will you produce that notebook?" Hamilton Burger thundered at Della Street.

"What notebook?" she asked.

"The notebook Norma Logan gave you Tuesday night," Hamilton Burger roared.

"Objected to," Perry Mason said, "as assuming a fact not in evidence. The Court has already ruled that any evidence as to anything received by Miss Street last Tuesday night is incompetent, irrelevant and immaterial, unless the prosecutor *first* shows it is connected with the issues involved in this case."

"I have assured the Court that it is! I have assured the Court on my honor as an attorney," Hamilton Burger shouted.

"I don't want your assurance," Mason said. "I'm representing the defendant John Kirby. The Constitution provides that he has the right to be confronted with the witnesses against him, and that he has the right to cross-examine those witnesses. If you want to have it appear in the record that this notebook is vital to the issues involved in this case, take the oath and get on the stand, and I'll cross-examine *you*, and prove that all *you* know about it is based on hearsay evidence."

Hamilton Burger started to say something, then found he had nothing to say. He glared at Perry Mason, then bent over to have a whispered conference with Sims Ballantine.

Abruptly Burger straightened, pointed his finger at Della Street, and said, "Did you have reason to believe, Miss Street, that a notebook you received last Tuesday night was connected with the murder of Dr. Phineas L. Babb, and pertinent evidence in the case of the People versus John Northrup Kirby?"

"Objected to," Mason said, "as calling for a conclusion of the witness, as argumentative and indirectly as calling for hearsay evidence."

158

Judge Cameron said, "Mr. Prosecutor, the Court is going to sustain the objection. Quite obviously you are going at the matter backwards. If it is your contention that this witness received any property from one Norma Logan, and that that property had in turn been stolen from the house of Dr. Babb, and was evidence in connection with this case, you're first going to have to show that in fact such a notebook has been stolen, that it is pertinent, and *then* you can ask this witness questions concerning it. But quite obviously you can't lay the entire foundation by examining this witness in this manner.

"Now the Court can appreciate that the circumstances are such that you may find them personally and officially exasperating, but nevertheless there's only one logical, orderly way to go about this thing, and in view of the objections which have been made by counsel, I am constrained to point out to you that you are adopting the wrong course."

"I'm going to fight it out on this line, if it takes all morning," Hamilton Burger shouted.

"Very well," Judge Cameron snapped.

"Last Tuesday night," Hamilton Burger said to Della Street, "you received property which you had reason to believe was evidence in this case, and you concealed that evidence, didn't you? Answer that question yes or no."

"Objected to," Mason said, "on the ground that it calls for a conclusion of the witness. The defendant in this case is not bound by what Miss Street may have *thought* she was receiving, provided she did receive anything. The defense in this case can only be bound by pertinent evidence which is introduced in an orderly manner, and shown to be connected with the case."

"The objection is sustained," Judge Cameron said.

"Well, Miss Logan gave you *something* Tuesday night, didn't she?"

"Objected to as incompetent, irrelevant and immaterial,"

Mason said. "It makes no difference what this witness may have received unless it was something that pertained to the present case."

"Sustained," Judge Cameron said.

Again Hamilton Burger had a whispered conference with his assistant.

Ballantine was gesticulating, explaining, while Hamilton Burger, flushed with anger, was quite evidently loath to follow the advice his assistant was giving him.

Judge Cameron said, "I think it is only fair to point out to you, Mr. District Attorney, that the Court has explained to you that there is no way you can prove this article to which you are referring is pertinent to the issues involved in this case unless this witness knows it of her own knowledge. You can't prove that by hearsay. It would certainly seem to me that the first step in a logical, orderly presentation would be to call Miss Logan as a witness."

"Very well," Hamilton Burger yielded with poor grace. "Step down, Miss Street. I'll call Norma Logan to the stand."

The courtroom buzzed with whispers, and Hamilton Burger, plainly exasperated to the point of apoplexy, slowly seated himself at the counsel table reserved for the prosecution.

Mason beckoned to Mrs. Kirby and, when she came forward, said, "Mrs. Kirby, I want you to sit here beside your husband."

Mrs. Kirby eased herself down into the chair which Mason drew up beside him.

"Will anyone object?" she asked.

"We'll wait and see," Mason whispered. "Now then, while I have you both together, I want you to know that I've put up with a lot in this case. I was retained to do what was necessary to protect the best interests of your son. I'm going to do it. I'm going to play the cards my own way. I'm—"

Mason stopped abruptly as Norma Logan came forward and raised her right hand. She took the oath and, quite evidently badly shaken, seated herself in the witness chair.

Hamilton Burger himself arose to conduct the examination. "You were acquainted with Dr. Babb during his lifetime?"

"Yes."

"On the night of Monday, the fifth of this month, did you go to the house of Dr. Babb?"

"Yes."

"Who took you there?"

"Mr. Kirby. He waited for me in his car."

"By Mr. Kirby, you mean the defendant in this case?"

"Yes, sir."

"And what did you do?"

"I went to Dr. Babb's office and entered and then took a seat in the waiting room."

"While you were at Dr. Babb's house, did you take any article of personal property without the permission of Dr. Babb?"

"Objected to," Mason said, "as incompetent, irrelevant and immaterial."

"I think you'll have to connect it up," Judge Cameron said. "I think a better foundation should be established."

"Very well," Hamilton Burger said. "I will ask you if you had occasion to enter the consultation office of Dr. Babb while you were there?"

"I did."

"And what was the occasion?"

"I heard a commotion and—" Suddenly the witness straightened on the witness stand. Her eyes became large and round. She raised a trembling forefinger, pointed it at

161

Mrs. Kirby, and shouted, "That's the woman! *That's the woman!*"

"Now, just a moment! Just a moment!" Judge Cameron said. "What's all this about?"

"That's the woman! That's the woman who murdered Dr. Babb!" the witness screamed, still pointing at Mrs. Kirby.

Hamilton Burger, in a frenzy of excitement, pushed forward to stand by the witness. "You mean *that's* the woman you saw in the room?"

"Yes, yes! The woman who was bending over Dr. Babb. That's the one who was in there!"

"Now, just a moment! Just a moment!" Hamilton Burger said. "I want to get this straight." He turned to the Court and said, "If the Court please, a situation has now developed that is totally unexpected. I would like to have permission of the Court to withdraw this witness temporarily until I can confer with her."

"Not before I've cross-examined her in connection with the statement she has just made," Mason said.

"Quite obviously," Hamilton Burger insisted, "this witness is emotionally upset. She is in no condition to be examined at the present time."

Mason said, "If the Court please, the prosecution's own witness has now identified another person as being the one who murdered Dr. Babb. This exonerates the defendant, John Northrup Kirby."

"Unless they acted together and in unison," Judge Cameron said. "Does the prosecution contend such is the case?"

"Very frankly," Hamilton Burger said, "the prosecution doesn't know."

"Well, if *you* don't know, you can't expect *us* to know," Judge Cameron said. "If you aren't satisfied there was a conspiracy or a joint undertaking, you're hardly in a position to ask the Court to bind the defendant over, in view of the statement which now comes from the lips of your own witness that Mrs. Kirby was the one who committed the murder."

"And," Perry Mason interpolated, "the witness has also testified that, at the time the murder was committed, the defendant in this case was sitting in a car some distance from the scene of the murder waiting for this witness to rejoin him."

"I don't think she has testified in quite that detail," Judge Cameron said, "but that would seem to be the effect of her testimony."

"Your Honor, if the Court please, *please*, Your Honor," Hamilton Burger said, "I want to withdraw the witness until she can become more composed. I would like to find out myself what this is all about."

"I can go on," Norma Logan said. "I was just upset. That's all. I haven't had any sleep and . . . and the shock of seeing that woman—"

"Just a moment," Judge Cameron said. "The Court will handle this. Just where did you see this woman, Miss Logan?"

"I went to Dr. Babb's office. I sat in the waiting room. I heard a commotion and the sound of a blow and a body falling, and then I heard a woman screaming. I ran to the door of the inner office and saw Dr. Babb lying the floor. I saw this woman bending over him."

"What did you do?" Judge Cameron asked.

"I stood there for a moment."

"Did she see you?"

"No, I'm satisfied she did not. She bent over Dr. Babb. The safe door was open and papers were scattered around over the floor. Then she dashed toward the back of the house."

"And then?" Judge Cameron asked.

"Then," she said, "I entered the room. I bent over Dr. Babb. I found he was still alive. I . . . I knew of one book in Dr. Babb's desk that I wanted. I took that book and ran with it."

"Where did you go?" Judge Cameron asked.

"I dashed down the street to where Mr. Kirby was waiting in his car."

"By Mr. Kirby you are referring to the defendant in this case?"

"Yes."

"And what did you do?"

"I got in the car and drove away with him. I told him what had happened and he took me down to a motel."

Judge Cameron said to the district attorney, "It would certainly seem, under the circumstances, Mr. District Attorney, that unless you are now prepared to prove some joint action on the part of husband and wife, your proof in this case shows that Mr. Kirby, the present defendant, must be innocent. As to whether his wife is guilty, that's another question. His wife is not formally before the Court at this time. She is not charged with anything."

Carver Kinsey, who had been sitting just inside the space reserved for attorneys, got up from his chair, hurried to Hamilton Burger's side and engaged in a whispered conference.

Hamilton Burger listened attentively, finally nodded, faced the judge.

"If the Court please," he said, "I'm trying to get this matter cleaned up, but since we now have the witness on the stand, I want to ask her one question. What did you do with that book which you took from Dr. Babb's office, Miss Logan?"

"Objected to as incompetent, irrelevant and immaterial," Perry Mason said. "It now appears from the prosecution's own witness that this defendant John Kirby must be innocent of any criminal act, except perhaps that of helping to conceal a witness. In view of the fact that he is not connected with the death of Dr. Babb, what this witness did with any property she might have taken from the home of Dr. Babb is absolutely immaterial as far as *this* defendant is concerned."

Judge Cameron frowned.

"If the Court please," Hamilton Burger said, "I want to be heard on this. Here is an important piece of evidence. Here is a piece of evidence which, in all probability, constituted the motivation for the murder of Dr. Babb. If that piece of evidence was delivered to the attorney for the defense or to his secretary, and has been willfully suppressed, that in itself is a breach of professional ethics and receiving that property, knowing that it had been stolen from the home of Dr. Babb, amounts to concealing stolen property, which is a felony."

"The Court will give Mr. Mason a chance to be heard," Judge Cameron said. "It would seem that the position of the district attorney is well taken."

"Suppose it is," Mason said, "what does it prove? It may prove a case against me, if that is the attitude the district attorney wants to take. But *I* am not on trial in this case. It certainly doesn't tend to prove anything against my client. It can't even prove anything against Mrs. Kirby. According to the testimony of the witness, Mrs. Kirby had already left the premises when this witness entered the private office and took the notebook from the desk. Mrs. Kirby can't be held responsible for something this witness did *after* she had left the premises, and certainly Mr. Kirby cannot be charged with any responsibility."

"I'm not charging Kirby with responsibility," Hamilton Burger bellowed. "I'm charging *you* with responsibility. I'm charging you with receiving stolen property."

"Go ahead and arrest me then," Perry Mason said.

"By heavens, I will!" Hamilton Burger shouted. "I now have the evidence. I'm going to sign a complaint personally charging you with receiving stolen property."

"Go ahead," Mason challenged.

"Now just a moment," Judge Cameron said. "We're going to keep this proceeding orderly. What are you going to do with the case against this defendant John Northrup Kirby, Mr. District Attorney?"

Hamilton Burger said, "I'm going to dismiss it. I—No, wait a moment, Your Honor, I'm going to get one matter straight before I do. I want to withdraw this witness from the stand and recall the witness Harvey Nelson who previously testified about Dr. Babb's dying statements. I think I know now what happened and I think I am prepared to clean up a corrupt mess which has existed at this bar for some time. Every case which Mr. Mason has handled has been presented with a dramatic fanfare of legal trumpets which has doubtless gratified Mr. Mason and surrounded him with the glitter of dazzling notoriety, but—"

"Now just a moment, Mr. Prosecutor," Judge Cameron interrupted. "We're not going to engage in personal abuse of counsel at this time. Address your remarks to the Court and refrain from inflammatory statements of this sort."

"Very well, if the Court please," Hamilton Burger said savagely, "I'll confine myself to the issues in the present case. I think we have witnessed a very cleverly played, in fact, a diabolically concocted scheme of—"

"Never mind that!" Judge Cameron said. "Specifically why are you addressing the Court?"

"I want to recall the witness Harvey Nelson."

"There seems to be no objection," Judge Cameron said. "Go ahead and recall him, and kindly refrain from these inflammatory statements. I may call your attention, Mr. Burger, to the fact that while certain aspects of the present case are what you might term flamboyantly dramatic, the entire drama has been the result of your own questions and your own conduct."

"All right," Hamilton Burger said. "I was tricked into a situation where this defendant and his counsel have received a temporary advantage, but I can assure the Court it will be short-lived."

"The Court has no interest in that matter whatever," Judge Cameron said. "The Court is interested in seeing that justice is done in an orderly manner. Therefore, if your remarks are addressed to the Court they are out of order, and if they were addressed to the representatives of the press, they were uncalled for. The Court has warned you on this matter, Mr. Prosecutor, and the Court does not intend to repeat that warning. The Court would suggest that you control yourself and either present this case or dismiss it."

"Call Harvey Nelson," Hamilton Burger said.

Nelson, who had been waiting at the swinging gate to the inner bar of the courtroom, pushed his way through and approached the witness stand.

"You've already been sworn," Hamilton Burger said. "Sit down there. Now Mr. Nelson, you made some comments about a statement made by Dr. Babb prior to his death when you asked him in the presence of witnesses if he knew who his assailant was and the doctor said he did and then mentioned a name."

"That is right," Nelson said.

"Now, in view of developments," Hamilton Burger said, "it occurs to me that the name *John* Kirby and the name *Joan* Kirby are sufficiently similar in sound so there could well have been a confusion in your mind. Is it possible that what the doctor actually said was Joan Kirby instead of John Kirby?"

"Just a moment," Mr. Mason said. "I object to the question on the ground that it is leading and suggestive, on the ground that it is an attempt to coach his witness while he is on the stand, that it is an attempt to put testimony in the mouth of the witness, that it is viciously leading, that it—"

"You don't need to go any further," Judge Cameron said. "The objection is sustained."

Hamilton Burger frowned. "I want to get this before the Court at this time," he said, "so that—"

"Before the *Court?*" Judge Cameron asked.

"Well, if the Court please, it's only fair to the public to understand the situation here."

"The Court has previously advised you, Mr. Burger, that you should present your testimony in an orderly manner and without regard to the press. Now the objection has been sustained. There's nothing before the Court. Do you want to ask another question, or have you finished?"

Hamilton Burger turned to engage in another whispered conference with Ballantine, then said, "I'll go at it in another way, Your Honor." He turned to the witness. "Mr. Nelson, you stated that the dying man made a statement to you as to the identity of his assailant."

"Yes, sir."

"Was that statement preserved in any way?"

"Yes, sir. It was."

"In what way?"

"On a tape recorder."

"And how was that done?"

"The microphone of a tape recorder was within a few inches of the lips of the dying man. The entire conversation was recorded on that tape recorder."

"Do you have that tape in your possession?"

"I do, but it is not with me at the moment."

"Can you get it?"

"Yes."

"And that tape shows exactly what was said?"

"It does."

"Then that tape is the best evidence, Your Honor," Hamilton Burger said, "and I have a right to have it played."

"I don't know whether it's the best evidence or not,"

Judge Cameron said, "but . . . is there any objection from the defense?"

"I would like to ask a question on cross-examination," Mason said.

"Very well, go ahead."

"You didn't tell us about this tape recording before."

"I wasn't asked."

"You deliberately refrained from mentioning it?"

"I didn't intend to mention it unless I was asked."

"Did someone give you instructions not to mention it unless you were asked?"

"Oh, Your Honor," Hamilton Burger said, "this is the same old seven and six, the same type of cross-examination, the same—"

"The district attorney will make specific objections and address his comments to the Court and refrain from criticizing counsel on the other side," Judge Cameron said. "The question is certainly well taken because it indicates the bias of the witness. The objection is overruled. Answer the question."

"Did someone tell you that?" Mason asked.

"Yes."

"Who?"

"Mr. Ballantine."

"By Mr. Ballantine, you mean the deputy district attorney here?"

"Yes."

"And what did he tell you?"

"He told me not to say anything about that tape recording unless I was interrogated concerning it. I have been interrogated on it now."

"All right," Mason said smiling. "Go and get the tape recording. We'll be very glad to hear it."

"This is going to take a few minutes, if the Court please," Hamilton Burger said. "May we have a thirty-minute recess?"

"Very well," Judge Cameron said. "The Court will take a thirty-minute recess. Now the Court is not entirely clear as to the admissibility of a tape recording made under such circumstances."

"It's the best evidence," Hamilton Burger said. "It records the sound itself."

"Is there any objection from the defense?" Judge Cameron asked Mason.

"None, Your Honor."

"Of course," Judge Cameron said, "in the present state of proof it now appears that the prosecution's own evidence indicates the innocence of the defendant."

"I know, I know, Your Honor. I'm just going at this thing . . . I want to go at it in my own way," Hamilton Burger said.

"The Court would like to point out that a proceeding before the grand jury is the proper manner in which to find out what happened in a case where the district attorney isn't certain. It is not the province of this Court to supervise a fishing expedition in trying to determine what actually did or did not happen."

"Yes, Your Honor," Hamilton Burger said, "if the Court will grant a thirty-minute recess and bear with me for a few moments, I think we can clear the matter up."

"Very well," Judge Cameron said, his manner showing an obvious dislike for tactics that quite plainly were designed to see that the inevitable dismissal of the case against John Kirby left the district attorney in the best possible light so far as newspaper publicity was concerned.

When the Judge had left the bench, John Kirby looked at his wife incredulously. "Joan, were you out there?" he asked.

"Yes," she whispered.

"But why in the name of reason—? How did you—?"

"That will do," Mason said. "People are watching you.

Just curtail your conversation. You're leaving things in my hands."

Kirby said grimly, "If you have that book, Mason, they'll get Ronnie. They'll get him and they'll get you. Damn it! They—"

"Take it easy," Mason interrupted. "I'm mapping the strategy in this case and I'll take care of myself."

Chapter 16

The scene in the courtroom was highly dramatic when Judge Cameron again took the bench at the end of the thirty-minute recess.

Harvey Nelson had set up a tape-recording device with an extension loud-speaker.

"Do you have the tape recording you have testified to?" Hamilton Burger asked the witness.

"I do."

"Will you please play that tape recording?"

Amidst tense, expectant silence, the machine gave forth a high-pitched hum. Suddenly from the loudspeaker came a voice so true to life that it startled the spectators. The amplified volume filled the courtroom.

"Dr. Babb, can you hear me? Can you hear me, Doctor? Dr. Babb, can you hear me?"

"Yes."

"Dr. Babb, do you know who hit you?"

"Dr. Babb, can you tell us the name of the person who hit you?"

There were several more repetitions of the question, then the answer, "Yes."

"Please give us the name. Doctor, please give us the name."

Again the question was repeated several times, and then in a slightly slurred tone of voice came the answer.

"That's all," Hamilton Burger said. "Shut off the machine."

Burger turned triumphantly to the Court. "It is quite

plain, now that we listen to it, that the name Dr. Babb gave is that of *Joan* Kirby, and not *John* Kirby."

"Please play that tape recording again," Judge Cameron said.

The witness played it once more.

"Of course," Judge Cameron pointed out, "in a matter of this sort, the imagination plays a part. The Court quite distinctly hears the name Kirby. Whether the first name is *John* or *Joan* is a question. The Court is very much inclined to think that the name is *John* Kirby rather than *Joan* Kirby."

"If the Court please," Hamilton Burger said, "making allowances for the fact that this man was injured, that there is a slight impediment in his speech, I think it is quite apparent that the name is Joan Kirby."

"Well," Judge Cameron said, "what's before the Court at this time?"

"I wanted to get this evidence into the record."

"I'm quite certain you did," Judge Cameron snapped. "But the case which you are *now* trying is the case of the People versus John Northrup Kirby. Now you are introducing evidence which you claim shows the dying man gave the name of the defendant's wife."

"I have not as yet excluded the possibility of a joint effort," Hamilton Burger said lamely.

"Well, you haven't any evidence which indicated it," Judge Cameron said. "Do you have any further questions of this witness?"

"No."

"Any cross-examination?" Judge Cameron asked Mason.

"No, Your Honor, I am assuming that the district attorney wishes to introduce this tape recording into evidence."

"Well, now, wait a minute," Hamilton Burger said. "We let the Court listen to the tape. I see no reason to have it introduced in evidence."

"That's the only way you can keep a record," Mason

said. "The court reporter can't transcribe the sounds that came from the tape recorder."

"He certainly can," Hamilton Burger said. "The name Joan Kirby is there as plain as can be."

"A few minutes ago, you were claiming it was the name John Kirby," Mason said.

Hamilton Burger showed his embarrassment.

"The Court thinks the tape should be introduced in evidence. It can subsequently be withdrawn, if necessary; but if it's part of the record, it should be in evidence," Judge Cameron said.

"Very well, Your Honor."

"Do you have any cross-examination of this witness?" Judge Cameron asked Mason.

"No, Your Honor."

"Call your next witness," Judge Cameron said to Hamilton Burger.

"If the Court please," Burger said, "I don't know whether we wish to dismiss this case against John Kirby or not. I would prefer to have a short time to think it over. Could we take a recess until two o'clock this afternoon?"

"Any objection on the part of the defense?" Judge Cameron asked.

Mason said, "I would like to recall one witness for further cross-examination if there is going to be continuance."

"Who is the witness?" Judge Cameron asked.

"The handy man who assisted Dr. Babb."

"Very well," Judge Cameron ruled. "The Court will refrain temporarily from ruling on the motion for a recess. Will the witness come forward please?"

The handy man came forward, took the witness stand.

Mason said, "I wanted to ask you one more question in view of the testimony of the witness Norma Logan that a woman ran out the back door. I believe there is an automatic door-closing device on the back door of Dr. Babb's house?"

"Yes, sir."

"Directing your attention to the place where you live over the garage, as I remember it there is a similar closing device and spring lock on your door. Is that correct?"

"Yes, sir."

"Now, then," Mason said, "when you left your apartment over the garage attired only in a towel, and dashed down to Dr. Babb's house, you found the back door of Dr. Babb's house closed and locked?"

"Yes, sir."

"You were attired only in a towel?"

"Yes, sir."

"And you have testified that the officers ordered you to go back to your quarters and wait there?"

"Yes, sir."

"Which you did?"

"Yes, sir."

Mason smiled. "Now," he said, "kindly tell the Court how it happened that, if you went down there attired only in a bath towel, if there is an automatic door-closing device on your door which causes it to swing shut, and if there is a spring lock on that door, how were you able to get back into your apartment? Who opened the door for you? Where did you have your key?

"And furthermore, Mr. Derby, I am going to ask you if, when the tape recording was played, and if, when you heard the voice of the dead man name the person who assaulted him, you didn't half get out of your chair with the intention of running from the courtroom because *you*, knowing Dr. Babb's voice better than anyone in the courtroom, heard him distinctly say that the name of his assailant was not John Kirby or Joan Kirby, but was Don Derby?"

Mason sat down.

Donald Derby started to say something; then found he had nothing to say. His face showed his utter consternation.

"And now," Mason went on with a little bow to the completely astounded district attorney, "I have no objection whatever to taking a recess until two o'clock this afternoon.

"In the meantime, I would suggest that, if you make a careful search of the clothes in the closet of Dr. Babb's house, you will find a suit of clothes in there which fits this witness but which wouldn't have fitted Dr. Babb. I think you will find a pair of shoes in there which wouldn't have fitted Dr. Babb. I think you will find socks, underwear and a shirt thrown into a corner of the closet or concealed in a bureau drawer.

"And by the time you have completed that investigation, you won't need to worry about pressing charges against Mrs. Joan Kirby, and in case you're still intending to file a complaint against me, charging me with receiving stolen property, you had better check with the public administrator, who will tell you that I have told him I was holding subject to his orders a notebook which I was informed had been taken from the house of Dr. Phineas L. Babb."

"You gave that book to the public administrator?" Hamilton Burger exclaimed incredulously.

"I am holding it subject to his order," Mason said, "and since Dr. Babb left no heirs, the public administrator is for the moment the real custodian of all the property. Therefore, instead of *receiving* stolen property, I have *recovered* stolen property, and am holding it for its rightful owner.

"Since you have seen fit to team up the resources of your office with the ideas of Mr. Carver Kinsey, I thought both of you would be interested to learn that the public administrator has signified a willingness to cooperate with me."

Burger took a deep breath. "You wouldn't have gone near the public administrator if it hadn't been for a *subpoena duces tecum* having been served on you and your secretary."

"Then," Mason said, "if you were trying so desperately

176

to trap me you should have refrained from serving the *subpoena duces tecum*, Mr. District Attorney."

Judge Cameron looked from one to the other, then looked to where Donald Derby was sitting in the witness chair. "Mr. Derby," Judge Cameron said, "can you answer that question propounded by counsel?"

"I don't have to," Derby said defiantly. "If they want to proceed against me, let them try and prove a case."

Judge Cameron turned to the district attorney. "Under the circumstances," he said, "the Court will take a recess until two o'clock this afternoon. I would suggest, Mr. District Attorney, that you take immediate steps to see that this matter is investigated, and this time I trust that it will be *competently* investigated."

Chapter 17

Perry Mason and Della Street regarded the curly-headed six-year-old child who stood quietly beside the chair occupied by Mrs. Kirby in Mason's office.

"I thought you'd like to see the one for whom you did all this work," she said.

"Hello, Ronnie," Mason said.

"Will you shake hands with Mr. Mason, Ronnie?"

Ronnie came forward, shook hands gravely with Perry Mason and bowed courteously to Della Street.

"Oh, you darling!" Della Street said, taking him suddenly into her arms.

When she released him, Ronnie backed away, apparently somewhat embarrassed by the effusive greeting, but still determined to be polite.

The door from the outer office opened, and John Kirby came in. "They told me you were in here and that I could come in," he said, "so here I am, checkbook in hand. Mason, can you ever forgive us for leaving you so much in the dark? We should have trusted you."

"It's always advisable to trust an attorney," Mason said dryly. "If you leave him in the dark he may kick something over."

"Well, Mr. Mason found his way through the dark all right," Mrs. Kirby said, "and when he turned on the light it certainly was a brilliant, dazzling light. The only thing is, I can't see why the police didn't know Dr. Babb said Don Derby instead of John Kirby."

"They were chasing too many red herrings," Mason said.

"Motley Dunkirk could have given them the key clue. In view of the fact that the man in Dr. Babb's office made a dash for the back door shortly after you screamed, it would appear that this man, whoever he was, should have been *seen* leaving the place.

"Mrs. Dunkirk was watching the door for some seconds *after* the screams. She saw no one. She went to the telephone to call the police some seconds after the screams had ceased. Her husband saw you emerge from the door. If the man ran when you started to scream, he must have left the building at a time when Mrs. Dunkirk would have seen him.

"That brought up the interesting possibility that he hadn't ever left the house, that he had deliberately concealed himself, hoping that you would run out of the back door just as you did, so that he could then return to the safe and get the book he wanted before the police arrived.

"Derby naturally assumed that you were going to call the police. He knew that he had relatively only a few seconds within which to accomplish his mission. Instead of running out of the back door when you screamed, he dashed into Dr. Babb's bedroom, closed the door and hurriedly divested himself of his wearing apparel. He had the foresight to take the key to his apartment out of his pocket before he hung his suit on a hanger in Dr. Babb's closet, kicked off his shows and socks, threw his underwear into a corner of the closet, and then dashed out to get the notebook that he wanted, a notebook with which he intended to make a fortune out of blackmail."

Della Street extended her hand to Ronnie. "Suppose we go look the offices over, Ronnie, while Mother and Daddy talk business with Mr. Mason? Do you want to?"

"Sure," Ronnie said smiling. "I like you. I'd like to go with you."

"Heartbreaker!" Della Street said as she gave him her hand and led him into the law library.

"Thanks to Paul Drake's excellent work in interviewing Steven Logan we can put together exactly what happened," Mason said.

"Steve Logan looked Dr. Babb up when the doctor started buying cars. For one thing, Steve was making a routine credit check, but over and beyond that Steve Logan knew that when his brother's second wife had been confined she had consulted Dr. Babb.

"Steve felt Dr. Babb was running some sort of a service and he wanted to know more about it. So he cultivated the handy man, talked with the doctor, and finally was ready to demand a showdown.

"The reason Dr. Babb didn't want to see Mrs. Kirby until late on that Monday night was that he already had an eleven o'clock appointment with Steve Logan. He wanted to try to find out just how much Logan was surmising. Also Dr. Babb intended to try to influence Steve Logan through Steve's niece, Norma, if he had to.

"So Steve Logan came to keep his appointment Monday night. Dr. Babb was talking with him, and when Mrs. Kirby came in several minutes before the time of her appointment, Dr. Babb was greatly concerned. He didn't want Steve Logan and Mrs. Kirby to meet. Norma had traced Ronnie to the Kirbys. Her uncle had only traced Ronnie to the doctor.

"Shortly before eleven o'clock, Dr. Babb had told Derby there would be nothing more for Derby to do that night and told Derby to go on up to his apartment. Derby pretended to do so, but instead of that had concealed himself in a closet in the inner office. He either knew something was in the wind and he had the idea of cutting himself in on a piece of cake, or else Steve Logan had bribed Derby to find out where Dr. Babb kept his records of babies whom he had placed in homes.

"Steve wouldn't admit that to Paul Drake, but I rather

180

have an idea that was the main reason for Derby's interest.

"After Steve Logan had left via the back door so Mrs. Kirby wouldn't see him, Dr. Babb just happened to open the closet door, discovered Derby, and so knew what was going on.

"Derby, knowing then that he was in for it, tried to get the records he wanted by simply overpowering Dr. Babb and grabbing them. Derby knew that once Dr. Babb had discovered his duplicity his job had gone out the window.

"Derby slugged his employer, and hit him too hard. He had turned to the safe when he heard Mrs. Kirby's screams. Alarmed and anxious to frame an alibi as well as to get one more chance at finding the book he wanted, he dashed toward the back door, but instead of leaving by that door, he detoured into Dr. Babb's bedroom, undressed and, hurriedly removing the key to his apartment from his clothes, grabbed a towel, wrapped it around his middle and made one more swift search for the book he wanted, a book which Norma Logan had already taken while Derby was undressing.

"He only had a few seconds. Then satisfied he couldn't find the book, he dashed out the back door and plunged into the goldfish pool so he would be all wet when the officers arrived. He barely made it.

"The officers, falling for his scheme, sent him up to his apartment to dress. Once up there he turned on the shower, made the wet footprints on the linoleum which the officers subsequently checked, then dried himself and dressed."

"But how did you first surmise all this?" John Kirby asked.

Mason said, "The key clue was the fact that a neighbor's cat was playing with a dead goldfish. The cat had never been able to catch a goldfish until that day.

"I wondered how the cat had managed to be so successful that one time, and then later on I suddenly realized that the cat hadn't caught the goldfish at all. Someone had jumped into the goldfish pool; that had caused a sudden overflow of water from the pool, and the fish had been swept out of the pool on the crest of this wave of water.

"It had flopped around on the ground until it had died, and there the cat found it the next day."

Kirby looked worried. "With all of this information floating around now, can you still protect our secret?"

"I think I can," Mason said, "if you'll just stop lying to me. We've come this far all right. I have some tricks left up my sleeve that I can use if I have to. Steve Logan made a statement to Paul Drake, but he's consulted a lawyer now and isn't saying a word at the moment."

"How can we ever apologize to you for not taking you into our confidence in the first place?" Kirby asked contritely.

"That," Mason said, "can be taken care of only by check. And," he added grimly, "don't think for a minute it won't be on the bill."

ERLE STANLEY GARDNER